MIDLOTHIAN LIBRARIES
D0277302

Also by Juan Marsé in English translation

Lizard Tails (2003)

Shanghai Nights (2006)

The Calligraphy of Dreams (2014)

JUAN MARSÉ

THE SNARES OF MEMORY

Translated from the Spanish by
Nick Caistor

MACLEHOSE PRESS
QUERCUS · LONDON

First published in the Spanish language as *Esa puta tan distinguida*
by Penguin Random House Grupo Editorial, S. A. U., Barcelona, in 2016
First published in Great Britain in 2019 by

MacLehose Press
an imprint of Quercus Editions Limited
Carmelite House
50 Victoria Embankment
London EC4Y 0DZ

An Hachette UK company

A CIP catalogue record for this book is available from the British Library.

ISBN (TPB) 978 0 85705 876 8
ISBN (Ebook) 978 0 85705 877 5

10 9 8 7 6 5 4 3 2 1

Designed and typeset in Cycles by Libanus Press
Printed and bound in Denmark by Nørhaven

Papers used by Quercus are from well-managed forests and
other responsible sources.

The only mask I'm wearing is the mask of time.
Mother Gin Sling, *Shanghai Nights*

Only you were thinking about murder.
And I was thinking about that anklet.
"Double Indemnity", based on the novel by James M. Cain

We have found the truth; and the truth makes no sense.
G. K. Chesterton, *The Innocence of Father Brown*

1 1 1

1) Here it is, señorita. Take it or leave it. I only give written replies.
2) Because I've always put more trust in writing than in pure blah-blah.
3) Adopted son of uncertain biological origin.
4) I'd have preferred to be born at another time, in another country, with blue eyes and a dimple in my chin.
5) Let's not waste time on nonsense. I don't militate under any banner. Flaubert used to say that they're all covered in blood and shit, and that it's high time we saw an end to them.
6) I am more than merely non-religious, I am resolutely anti-clerical. Until the Catholic Church begs forgiveness for its complicity with Franco's dictatorship, declaring myself anti-clerical is the least I can do. I

have enjoyed a healthy phobia of the clergy since early adolescence.

7) The only clerics I respect are Father Pietro in *Rome, Open City* by Rossellini, the Nazario of Galdós and Buñuel, Chesterton's Father Brown and the raging, dishevelled Irish priest in David Lean's *Ryan's Daughter*.
8) I lost this finger when I was fifteen. It was chewed up in a rolling mill.
9) Music. I'd have liked to be Glenn Gould's piano or Charlie Parker's sax.
10) My next novel will deal with the tricks and snares created for us by memory, that high-class whore.
11) No. If I tell you what it's about, I'll spoil it, because this novel is a kind of *trompe-l'oeil*. Nothing in it is what it seems, starting with the title.
12) Well, what I have currently been commissioned to write isn't exactly what could be called literature. I'm working on the first treatment of a film script.
13) Yes, for money.
14) I hate talking about my work. But basically it involves an elderly murderer, apparently suffering from Alzheimer's, who tells the story of his crime thirty years after he committed it. He can remember that he killed a prostitute but has absolutely no memory of why.
15) I don't have a title. It might be *The Killer's Forgetfulness* or *The Mask and Amnesia*, or something of the

sort. It's about the persistence of desire and the strategies of forgetting.

16) I intend to base the story on real events: a very famous and often fraudulent claim, I must admit.

17) With few exceptions, a film script is not written to be read as a work of literature, whose material and basic premise is language. A script is a text to be used and thrown away.

18) The producer and director are the ones in charge, but you have to consider the vagaries of our feeble film industry. The project could end up in the hands of a different producer, with a different commercial emphasis: it could end up as a spaghetti western, a horror movie, soft porn, or a farce. (N.B. Not a film that makes people laugh, but one that people laugh at).

19) During the interminable dictatorship, our nationalist-Catholic pasteboard cinema gave rise to such dire moral and artistic poverty, took such great delight in its own falsity and stupidity, that it was many years before we could raise our heads again. Things have improved, of course. But now there's a different problem, and it's universal: technology is killing cinema.

20) With a girl called María. I was fifteen and she was eighteen.

21) I couldn't give a damn about national identity. It's an emotional swindle. I'm a poor, unpaid patriot.

22) No. The writer's true homeland is not his mother tongue, but language itself.

23) My vocation as a writer was born on the corner of Calles Bruc and Valencia outside the Barcelona Music Conservatory. I must have been about fourteen at the time. A young girl student who was standing by the entrance with a violin case under her arm asked me to go in with her and say to her teacher: "It was me." She didn't tell me what that meant, and I didn't ask. "I'll explain later," she said with a sweet smile. I went in, did the strange favour she had asked, and left at once. As agreed, I waited for her out in the street, but she never re-emerged, and I never saw her again. I was left wondering what lay behind my self-accusation: I couldn't stop thinking about it, so much so that I began to fantasise about a possible emotional conflict involving the two of them. I imagined a passionate love story between the beautiful girl and her handsome teacher, a secret passion encoded in the enigmatic phrase: "It was me." I like to think that the imaginative effort I made at fourteen based on those three words was the origin of my vocation.

24) I haven't the faintest idea what you're talking about.

25) Let's see, I'll try to explain it another way. The suspicion that there was a tumultuous passion between the youthful teacher and his beautiful student became

an obsession, and the only way to free myself from it was to express it verbally. That was how it started, that's how the novice writer felt the birth of a vocation: the need to tell the story. Is that clear now?

26) In my fictions, real experience is ruled by the imagination, which is more rational and credible. The invented part contains my more truthful autobiography.
27) What's that? I'll never write a novel about the crisis of social structures. Who do you take me for?
28) Culture? The politicians in this country don't give a shit about culture; that's why they leave it to decrepit old fogies.
29) What the novel needs today is fewer adjectives and more substantives.
30) The real character I most admire? Emma Bovary.
31) Fictional character? Carmen Balcells.
32) I'm very happy with my agent and would never change her for anyone else. Besides, what would be the point? At my age, changing my literary agent would be like moving deckchairs on the last night of the *Titanic*.
33) I turned down the offer. Like Groucho Marx, I would never want to belong to a Royal Academy of the Language that would have me as a member.
34) I only trust the logic contained in good music.
35) I don't recognise myself in live interviews. I don't recognise my voice.

36) Again? I detest any kind of nationalism. The homeland that nationalists offer is sentimental carrion.

37) Nietzsche predicted it: with another century of newspapers, words will become pernicious.

38) I'd exchange all this for a Cole Porter song.

39) I'd give the whole film for one shot by John Ford.

40) Pass.

41) Too verbose to be memorable, too intellectual to be moving. He's a notable writer, but not a good novelist. In a good novelist, what shines isn't the intellect, it's something else. I'd swap the entire book for a page of Dickens.

42) In my novel, there is a murderer but no criminal investigation. I'm not a faddish writer recycling myself as a blasted author of noir fiction. There is no psychopath to uncover or arrest. The murderer, *c'est moi*!

43) The only things I regret are those I have left undone. As the poet wrote: what I haven't done, what I don't do, what I am failing to do at every moment. That's what I regret.

44) What I envied at the age of fifteen was the way Clark Gable waggled his eyebrows.

45) I write to know whether I really have been the protagonist of my life, like David Copperfield.

46) When I finished writing that book I felt very

depressed. I was satisfied with the different parts, but disconcerted by it as a whole. I felt as if the plot had been stolen from me, the nub of the storyline.

47) Forget that and remember what Nabokov said: "There's no point reading a novel unless it's with your marrow. Even though you read with the mind, the crux of artistic enjoyment can be found between the shoulder blades, a tingling of the marrow in the spine."

48) That's more than enough, señorita. Good night.

2

In mid-June 1982 I took on a commission to write a script based on a true event that had occurred years earlier in Barcelona, a horrendous murder that at the time gave rise to many different theories, a crime whose motive was never adequately explained. The fateful event took place in the projection booth of a local cinema in January 1949; it's still remembered today as a great mystery. The murderer's immediate confession and subsequent amnesia, the gruesomeness of some of the details, and in particular the voluptuous atmosphere surrounding the victim, a prostitute strangled with a collar of celluloid – a length of film cut from one of the two films showing that week – a film whose title does not appear in the case files I was able to consult, but which I recalled because its heady erotic perfume wafted through my adolescence – were aspects of the affair regarded as highly important by the producer and the director when they offered me the job.

Back then, both of these men enjoyed considerable prestige and solid reputations in the industry. The producer was a powerful, much-feared wheeler-dealer by the name of Moisés Vicente Vilches. The director was Héctor Roldán, a leading light in the most international Spanish cinema of the 1950s, whose black-and-white filmography was highly critical of the dictatorship and was brave and well-meaning, though I have to confess the films were also boring as hell. His ideological blinkers undermined his undoubted talent, to the point where all the protest films of his that were once so lauded now seem full of trite political drivel, textbook leftist orthodoxy and militant Communist Party resonances that set one's teeth on edge. Roldán had always flirted with pamphleteering, and, as I could tell when he explained his new project to me, he was intent on affording himself that pleasure yet again.

In those days, the summer of 1982, the whole country was torn between memory and forgetting. Everything was shifting, and Héctor Roldán knew it. He was an intelligent man, but his raised fist had become frozen because he insisted on the same cheap political slogans that had once brought him success: he wanted the sordid story of the crime in the Delicias cinema to be a film reflecting the moral and political turpitude of the Franco regime, buried four years earlier when we embarked on the transition to democracy. An admirable proposal, but . . .

"I see," I told him. "A therapeutic film."

"I don't know what you mean . . ."

"A film with a nutritious supplement of nuts and carrots that are good for the memory." The intense film director could not see the funny side of that and did not laugh. "Well, anyway: are you sure I'm the right person to write it?"

"I have my reasons for thinking you are."

He went on to explain that this reflection of reality would subtly underpin the plot, and suggested I would not find that strange or hard to achieve, since I had already shown I was well aware of it and, in fact, it had featured prominently in my early and best novels, the ones "of social protest that I had the chance to read in prison". This was the backhanded praise he gave me, but in fact it was aimed at himself, a way of boasting how he had been harassed and mistreated by the Franco regime. This explained the doubtful privilege of my being chosen to write the first treatment of the script, or "narrative pretext" as he termed it. In his view, I was the perfect person to lay the foundations for the story because the crime took place in the "vivid urban setting" of my literary fictions; in other words, in the territory of my adolescence, on my streets and involving a humble local cinema that I used to frequent – one that was not even grand enough to put on re-runs – and above all because the event had already appeared, dealt with very freely and indirectly, and of course without any direct political intention ("a big missed opportunity, a real shame") – in one of my novels published six years earlier, after originally being banned by the regime's censorship. I saw no point in telling him that good films, like good novels, have as much direct political intent as those old comics, *Hipo, Monito y Fifi*, or fairy tales – in other words, none at all – so I tried to make a joke with a double-edged compliment:

"Yes, but time waits for no man, Mister DeMille."

"Of course, of course, there's lots of stale celluloid," he conceded, tacitly accepting the sarcastic nickname. "Nowadays we're living a new era, we're inaugurating democracy and new freedoms. There's no denying that. Which is why all we have to do is tell the facts as they are. The incontrovertible, undeniable facts. That's enough: the demagogy of fact."

"Well, the facts are very confused. Everything about this crime is very confused . . ."

"So much the better!" he at once replied, a sudden glint in his senile eyes. "Because everything that's confused, complex and absurd needs to be at the heart of our story, my friend, the story we are really going to tell, the one that takes us beyond the mere plot. The loss of meaning, of any real awareness of things, that's what I want to show in my film! And in order to tell it, the plot and montage are superfluous, if you follow me. We're going to replace plot with naked reality."

After making such an outlandish statement *à la* Antonioni, to use the kind of turn of phrase typical of my assistant Felisa, an insufferable film buff, the worthy veteran director sat back, looking pleased with himself. When I replied that reality never appears to us as naked, he retorted that there were no witnesses to the crime and that the official version established temporary insanity as the determining cause for the murder, an absurd, inexplicable fit of fury, the alleged sequel to a previous and equally inexplicable attempt by the murderer to steal money and jewels from the victim. "A load of nonsense!" he exclaimed, because the truth was that the prostitute was wearing only a pair of cheap earrings. He insisted that our script should pick up on and emphasise such a pathetic distortion by the police and judiciary, filled with unsubstantiated accusations, suspicions and downright lies, since it would be thanks to these deliberate twists to the official version that we would succeed in taking the film beyond an indictment of the regime. Because that was what it was all about, he insisted, going far beyond a simple indictment.

"Those are the illusions, the rainbow-coloured soap bubbles that the Franco regime has left us, and we're going to pop them," he added. "But first things first. For now, what they want from you is a detailed description of the behaviour of the murderer and the victim prior to the crime. I want more than a storyline, I want a faithful chronicle of how the crime in that booth was committed: in other words, a painstaking, minute-by-minute account, including dialogue if you think that's necessary and if there are true and reliable references to what was said . . . In reality, and let me insist on this so that it's crystal clear, what we are after is not a plot as such, so don't waste your time on that. I don't need any fictional narrative logic this time, or any stupid intrigue, a criminal investigation you can find in any thriller, because here there's no murderer to uncover."

He went on to say that he was well aware of my coincidental closeness to the terrible event, a geographical closeness at least, since as a boy I had been a neighbour and doubtless an acquaintance of one of the real-life characters in the drama, a deranged member of the Falange, a local councillor by the name of Ramón Mir Altamirano (who appeared anonymously in one of my early short stories and turned up again twenty years later in a novel of mine), the man who, as was revealed during the trial, was a lover of the murdered woman and had led her into prostitution. I told him that back then everyone, starting with his own wife, took him to be an irredeemable braggart, a bully who had a screw loose and in fact ended up completely nuts. Besides, I said, I had no recollection of ever having exchanged so much as a single word with him, even though we lived almost next door to each other. And I warned Roldán:

"It's true the crime took place in my neighbourhood, but that doesn't mean you can expect any special insights from me, much less for me to be emotionally involved in the story. I had heard of this Mir fellow; I think he often abused his position as a councillor and member of the Falange. But I never spoke to him, and now couldn't say whether I passed him on the street more than half a dozen times . . . In those days

I was a kid who lived with his head in the clouds. Or rather, on Barcelona's bald mountain."

Roldán was enchanted by my scornful emotional distancing from the event. He told me that this outsider's viewpoint was an ideal way to approach the subject. He insisted that, rather than develop a plot, what he really wanted to achieve with this film was to "emphasise the absurdity of the crime, demolish any trace of a conventional plot and shake the audience to the core". Hearing this, I was filled with all sorts of doubt. For heaven's sake, by then I had more than enough reasons to fear the worst from pompous, incompetent film-makers, because I knew what they were capable of. And yet in this instance I told myself: Take the money and run, we'll sort things out later.

In short, if eventually I had a proper understanding of the idea, what was required of me was a more or less step-by-step report on what led both the murderer and his victim to the drama that reached its climax in that projection booth: a truthful, non-judgmental and journalistic account of their final hours, bearing in mind above all that the film's only message, according to the director's express wish (although this would only be made clear in the definitive version, which Roldán himself would write), was that, above and beyond the dubious motive cooked up by the police and the judiciary, which even in 1949 convinced no-one and gave rise to all kinds of conjectures and rumours, what had to be stressed was this original hypothesis: whatever emotions might have led to the crime, loving passion or hate, madness, revenge, or simple larceny, once the bubbles had burst, the two protagonists, the whore and her murderer, should appear clearly as victims of the political system and as the only ones who had lost out.

"Isn't that a plot though?" I said.

"It's nothing more than a consequence," Héctor Roldán said. "The logical consequence of institutionalised depravity on a national scale that affected every one of us, at all levels of society, and from which no-one could escape. I don't know if you follow me."

"Oh, indeed I do."

This well-meaning denunciation of our national depravity and victimisation, likely to be illustrated on screen by concepts rather than characters, in other words by abstract rather than lived experiences, sounded very familiar to me. I had often heard it before. It even made me prick up my film-loving ears, like the resonant ring of a bicycle bell. And although, as I had just learned, I would not be the one to give the final version of the script that decisive socio-political message, I could imagine the end product: it was akin to the movie where an anonymous cyclist is run down on a highway, except that here there would be no cyclist and no highway, only a strangled whore instead of an unfaithful wife crashing her car and receiving her just reward. The prospect could not have been more depressing: we had all seen that movie, and its message, recycled almost thirty years later in the midst of Spain's political transition thanks to Héctor Roldán, could turn into a visual artefact as wooden as it was obsolete.

We finally agreed I should start work using a copy of the case files and for the moment stick strictly to the proven facts, the declarations of the murderer himself as well as the record of the court proceedings. Later on we would go over the material together, and, following his suggestions, establish a definitive shooting script.

For his part, before returning to Madrid, the producer M. V. Vilches, perhaps to allay my fears as to the director's suspect intentions and his alarming aesthetic preoccupations (made worse, let it be said in passing, by a jarring affectation in his choice of shots), tried to convince me that this time, in his new film, the combative director was aiming only for professional recognition, that of a good storyteller in images, and had nothing to do with any other consideration or merit, even his well-known emphasis on a particular ideology . . .

"Like hell!" I said to myself. "This fellow will never stop being the most virulent and distinguished boil on the left buttock of Spanish cinema's scrawny arse."

Be that as it may, and to be completely frank, yours truly here, let down more than once by the insipid film adaptations of some of my books, could not have cared less about the persistent, castrating ideological preferences of the director, especially since I had once espoused them myself. Thinking it over, the transgressive spirit this man had shown in difficult times was at least worthy of respect.

I asked a lot of money for my involvement – much more than I usually did – and they agreed. At that moment, I wouldn't have minded if they had refused. Years earlier when I had taken on this kind of work, I had hoped to be able to establish a creative complicity, however minimal, with the director (I must say that this was always in vain, except for a single project I really cared about, which never came to fruition), by putting myself at the service of his ideas and talent from the outset. But on this occasion, when Roldán called me, I had long since abandoned such ridiculous expectations, so that from the start I was not particularly bothered about the result, and it goes without saying that the success or failure of the film was all the same to me. After all, why should I worry if yet again the final product was out of my hands? All I had to do was to gather as much information as possible, and construct a story based on true events.

There was no trustworthy hypothesis about what had actually happened: the police and judicial investigations back in 1949 could only offer an incomprehensible mishmash of conjecture and speculation, and the sensationalist press reports I consulted – all of them restricted by the severe censorship of the time – were equally unforthcoming. The information available about the lives of the two main protagonists in the hours leading up to the crime was almost non-existent, which gave me a chance to explore various theoretical avenues without exhausting any of them, and to offer an open ending that the director would like, as he was insisting on rejecting any tricks or a linear plot.

"First and foremost," Roldán had told me, "you need to gather everything you can about the victim and her murderer. Their backgrounds, by which I don't mean their police records, but their personal lives in the four or five days, or perhaps weeks, whatever it takes, leading up to the crime."

"O.K."

"What they were doing, how they lived and where, how they fitted in to that spectral, starving Barcelona of the post-war years. I need the atmosphere, the colour and sounds of those days of shame in this city."

"O.K."

"And you need to faithfully recreate the scene of the crime." His eyes glinted once more. "A projection booth in a local cinema, what could be more enticing! The sound of the projector whirring! A stack of film reels! Tremendous! I can already smell the nitrate and acetone! I can smell it!"

"O.K., O.K. Where do I sign?"

I began work. I gathered reports, files, court proceedings and a whole series of statements. But the problems soon became obvious. The original documentary intention was a drawback and a nuisance: the facts did not stand out enough to make them memorable. They did not seem credible. I had very little information about the hours immediately preceding the crime, while the murderer's statements, from what I could gather from his confession to the police and the trial records, were always confused, if not downright contradictory. While he was being held in jail prior to the trial, he insisted time and again that he had experienced several panic attacks that led him to try on three occasions to commit suicide and caused a serious mental block. This meant he ended up in the hands of an eminent military psychiatrist who was experimenting with new methods – something that seemed to me extremely important. In order to prevent him going mad or committing suicide, this doctor had made him undergo intensive therapy designed to make him forget the rush of blood that led to his terrible act. This therapy apparently had some success, with the result that when the trial took place, the accused could remember all the details of the crime but not the reason for it. This bolstered the approach taken by his defence: the cause of the crime was a sudden, inexplicable fit of madness, an impulse without rhyme or reason. The final verdict was very clear: the convicted, self-confessed killer Fermín Sicart Nelo could recall perfectly how he had killed the prostitute Carolina Bruil Latorre, but had absolutely no idea of why he had done so.

A careful reading of the trial proceedings revealed a certain indulgence of the court towards the forgetful prisoner, with very little attention paid to some judicial procedures, not to mention the hasty, confused conclusions as to the motive for the crime. As the killer confessed during his psychiatric examination, the prostitute's last words, pronounced seconds before she died, were "hurry up". This was not the only intriguing detail I found in the court records. The fact is that the whole case looked suspiciously like a cover-up, a sham possibly cooked up by the sinister Politico-Social Brigade, to conceal something that might affect some bigwigs higher in the chain of command. This might have been a fantasy on my part, but it was doubtless one that would suit Héctor Roldán down to the ground: it could be one of those toxic bubbles he was so keen to pop.

I had already scribbled twenty or so pages based on the court reports and the killer's own confession, but my growing suspicion that the police file was a tissue of falsehoods and distortions led me to want to invent things, and this made me uneasy. I was worried about working in this ill-defined frontier between fiction and testimony, and it was not long before I was fed up to the back teeth with everything being so hazy, unclear and hypothetical. I needed to discover the main thrust of the plot, or what seemed closest to a plot, or at least a certain symmetry or harmony that would energise the story and would mean that, however trivial or strange it might seem (the truth or otherwise of it seemed to me irrelevant), the rest of the film could take on life and meaning. Above all, what on earth moved the killer's hands, what motivated him, what induced him to strangle a prostitute whose services he had asked for by calling a telephone number in a bar on the Rambla? Was it really a case of momentary madness? If so, it might be interesting to explore that avenue, even from the no-plot point of view the director wanted. And yet . . .

To resolve my doubts I read the file once more and took a pile of notes, in a vain attempt to discover a thread that might allow me to establish a minimal sequential logic.

Police Headquarters. VIth Regional Brigade for Social Investigation.

Police record of Carolina Bruil Latorre. Files B-7 (14-02-45) and B-8 (17-03-49). Summary for internal use only.

Born Teruel, 5 April 1917. Moves to Barcelona at age 18 to go into service; shortly afterwards enters the entertainment business on Avenida Paralelo as dancer and contortionist. In summer 1940 begins to make a name for herself appearing in variety shows at venues (Cinema Selecto and Cinema Moderno) under the stage name of "Chen-Li" or "the Chinese Girl". Later on, appears semi-naked in a highly indecent revue called "Puss in Boots". No charges against her.

Married in 1938 to someone calling himself Jesús Yoldi Pidal, aged 35, employee in a film distribution company and actor in an amateur theatre group in Gràcia, based at 106 Calle Ros de Olano. According to file B-6 (03-05-44) suspected of assuming a false identity. Real name thought to be Braulio Laso Badía, leading activist of banned C.N.T. union with several cases pending, current whereabouts unknown. Laso Badía regarded as one of the founders of the clandestine C.N.T. Entertainment Union, responsible for the printing and distribution of articles and subversive propaganda in cinemas. Warrant for his capture and arrest dating from the beginning of current year.

In spring 1945, with Braulio Laso Badía still in hiding, his supposed wife, Carolina Bruil Latorre, begins an adulterous relationship with Ramón Mir Altamirano (henceforth R.M.A.), ex-combatant of the Blue Division and city councillor for the La Salud district. On 28 May 1945, a month after the start of this relationship, the so-called Jesús Yoldi Pidal, alias Braulio Laso Badía, is found hanged under the pergola of a flat roof on Calle Legalidad, in a property owned by a friendly couple who had offered him food and shelter since the warrant for his arrest. Suicide put down to a fit of despair on learning of his wife's adultery (this is unconfirmed).

A year later, at an unknown date, Carolina Bruil Latorre, while continuing to appear in variety shows, starts occasionally to work as a prostitute, apparently at the instigation of her lover, R.M.A. She loses a son aged 11 from tuberculosis, and becomes increasingly dependent on alcohol. Eventually completely abandons acting and becomes a full-time prostitute, frequenting bars and other locales at the lower end of the Rambla. Never worked in a brothel, always on her own account. Still associated with R.M.A.

The following details are taken from statements by the self-confessed murderer Fermín Sicart Nelo (Case Files F-16 and F-17, 23-01-49) confirmed by subsequent inquiries.

On 23-04-45, as part of the investigation into Liberto Augé Dalmau, aged 59, bachelor, usher at the Delicias cinema, an individual with the extreme, outlandish elegance and fussiness of a pervert, Fermín Sicart Nelo, aged 26, cinema projectionist, a colleague of said Dalmau, is interviewed under caution. Sicart Nelo declares he has no knowledge of the illegal activities of either Augé Dalmau or Yoldi Pidal, and is unaware of the possible double identity of the latter, whom he claims to have met only once, and with whom he denies having any political or ideological links. He further alleges he knows nothing about leaflets or anarchist publications concealed in the sacks of film reels that he receives for projection, sacks which are bundled up and distributed from one cinema to another. The responsibility for these activities apparently lies with the aforementioned Augé Dalmau, alleged member of the clandestine union of the banned C.N.T., an individual with a long history in the organisation and diffusion of said subversive propaganda. The projection booth of the Delicias cinema was searched in the presence of the projectionist Fermín Sicart, prior to his transferral to Police Headquarters for interrogation, but no evidence was found. Sicart Nelo was released, whilst Augé Dalmau, known as "The German", who displayed obvious signs of a probably shameful homosexuality (unconfirmed), was put under close surveillance.

There are indications that Augé Dalmau could have been

involved in the anarchist plot that in July 1947 led to the vile murder of Eliseo Melis, an informer who offered such good and loyal service to the VIth Brigade. Unconfirmed.

In September 1947, the prostitute Carolina Bruil Latorre, now known as "Carol", begins an intimate relationship with said Fermín Sicart Nelo, assistant projectionist at the Delicias cinema, to whom she from time to time grants sexual favours in his workplace.

It appears that in this cinema the main projectionist and part-time usher is Liberto Augé Dalmau (Files C-3/ 12-04-39 and C-4/ 21-03-45), friend and suspected accomplice of the deceased Braulio Laso Badía (alias Jesús Yoldi Pidal). It is here that the events described below took place.

On the evening of 11 January 1949, Carolina Bruil Latorre pays a visit to her lover and client Fermín Sicart Nelo at the Delicias cinema, and is murdered by him in the projection booth by strangulation. The forensic report ascribes the cause of death to asphyxia and details marks of strangulation by lengths of film with sharp edges that caused wounds to the neck.

During his initial interrogation, the murderer alleges he is suffering from a mental block and cannot remember what drove him to commit the crime.

Psychological Report (Colonel Tejero-Cámara, 29-01-1949)

In view of the number of unanswered questions and the additional evidence available for consideration, such as the accused's erratic memory regarding the motive for the crime and regarding the twenty-four hours leading up to it, in addition to the forensic report (14-01-1949), the conclusion of the initial psychological examination is that the reason for the crime could have been a sudden, unexpected moment of madness whose consequences the accused did not foresee . . .

Dazed as I was by this jumble of indigestible prose, meaningless dates and possibly manipulated information, Carolina Bruil appeared to me as though lit by a flash of lightning as she swayed her hips with unconvincing coquettishness, a calculated simpering, as if she were awkwardly attempting to seduce an uncouth client . . . The various versions of this scene that I scribbled down when they were more or less of no use to me now seem like a real epiphany: there she is, sprawled on a pile of film-reel cans in the darkest corner of the projection room, wearing black stockings and with her raincoat around her shoulders, a mortadella roll in one hand and in the other a bottle of wine kindly provided by the projectionist, smiling as she says "Hurry up," but unable to conceal a deep-seated sadness, a resigned acceptance that foreshadows the end. She lays the bottle and the food on top of the cans, picks up the snaking roll of film from the floor, drapes it around her neck and then, with a gesture now so often seen it has lost all its power of seduction, sways her hips and extends one leg, offering a glimpse of her thigh between the folds of her coat.

Seconds before the sharp edge of the celluloid starts to cut into her throat, she knows she is going to die, and slowly and sorrowfully closes her ash-grey eyes. For one brief moment, beyond her weary exhortation and his violent response, both victim and murderer appear to sense that something fateful is about to take place. Because it is not only desire or chance or loneliness that has brought them together this rainy January evening in such an incongruous setting for sexual intercourse, a dark hole smelling of nitrate . . .

Steady on, you're not being paid to create mysteries, still less to pursue them like this, I told myself over and over. And yet the prostitute's crude sexual reference, which had initiated a silent drama, the prelude to the brutal murder, was an image whose meaning at that moment escaped me, but which I liked to think could end up being crucial: an image that would not merely be an aesthetic jewel (the most persistent temptation in Héctor Roldán's films) but would create the primordial urge of a mysterious emotional catharsis. But like so many others, this supposition was premature. The imagined shot froze on my retina, and I stored it away along with everything else.

3

Fortunately I had time to shirk the task in hand, and so I decided to alternate the tragic story of Carolina and Fermín with a personal project I was much more enthusiastic about: to return to the second draft of a novel that had been progressing laboriously over the previous six months, with frequent dry periods that gradually became ever more frequent, to the extent that the draft ended up abandoned in a drawer and would only be rescued some twenty-five years later. It involved a complex fictional narrative that had nothing to do with any godforsaken commission and which from time to time allowed me to forget the film and recover some dignity and decency in my writing. But that was only occasionally: as I have admitted already, recently not even in my own writing have I found words easy to come by. For some reason, when evoking the past, I still felt the weight of a castrating official censorship that paradoxically by 1982 no longer existed: the insidious injunction not to call things by their name. It was as if certain words that had been avoided and stored away for too long were still affected by the plundering and disrepute suffered for so many years, so that they suddenly lost their point of reference and changed meaning – they hid their true significance and treacherously turned their backs on me. I had the impression I was painfully dragging them up one by one from the depths of a black well. The words were there on paper, and yet they remained in disguise, looking in another direction and persisting in their falsity. At moments such as these I was engulfed by the feeling that the words I needed, the precise and relevant ones, the essential ones, the only words of any value to me, those that would not leave me helpless when faced with the blank page, were still at the bottom of the well poisoned by censorship and disdain. Those experiences and emotions that had been unnameable and buried in silence for so long, those words condemned right up to the previous day to a dictatorial muteness, and which now could and should be resolutely summoned without fear of reprisal, those words insisted on maintaining their air of falseness, betraying the meaning that lay behind them.

This was the feeling of impotence I was filled with that hot July evening, after five hours chained to my desk staring at half a dozen handwritten pages. It was a time when many things and the words that signified those things were not yet fully reunited. I ought to add that I am not talking about a work of testimony or a risky, important indictment that a threatened writer might have kept in a bottom drawer for years, waiting till after the fall of the Franco regime to publish it, and which when the day finally arrives to expose it to the light of freedom is suddenly seen to be neither important nor a testimony, or to run any kind of risk, because inevitably it's made up of words which were unable, even in clandestinity and behind the back of the censors, to free themselves from being hollowed out, distorted or self-deceiving. No, it was none of that. I'm talking about a draft written only the day before that was behaving treacherously, as if it had been composed at the height of the dictatorship: underhand, sly, aphasic, the words remained only vague. I resolved to turn eyes and mind away from their jangling falsehood and blandness, and, doubtless to somehow counteract such unrelenting verbal deficiency, the syndrome left over from almost forty years of self-censorship (in my imagination at least, although I'm conscious of my stubborn inadequacies), decided to play an innocent if rather crude joke on our family's elderly assistant.

"Felisa," I said, putting on a doom-laden voice, "when the murderer arrives, show him onto the terrace. Give him a beer and ask him to wait for me."

Felisa had just come into my study, broom in hand, on the pretext of wanting to sweep the parquet floor as she did every afternoon, even though today she knew it was spotless because she herself had vacuumed it only three hours earlier. She listened to my instructions, leant her hands and chin on the broom handle, and stared at me with her wide, all-seeing eyes. Perhaps "murderer" was a word that had been emptied of meaning for her too. A few hours before, when I informed her I was expecting an important visitor and was encouraging her to make sure there were enough beers and soft drinks in the fridge, I didn't consider it necessary or wise to add that my expected caller, Señor Fermín Sicart, had strangled a woman more than thirty years earlier. But now, when I sprung on her the fact that he was a murderer, it would only have been natural for her to be startled, or at least show some sign of surprise or simple curiosity. But my far from subtle little joke, an innocent distraction permitted to a vocational chatterbox who has wasted an entire afternoon scribbling away, had no effect whatsoever. Without reacting in any way, her cigarette burning down between the mocking corners of her mouth, and with her hands firmly clasped around the top of the broom, my assistant treated me to the habitual, moist, slow droop of her large grey eyes, a sly, malevolent look that not even Bette Davis in her pomp could have matched.

"With the glass chilled or at room temperature?"

"How should I know? Whatever he prefers. He probably likes his beer cold," I said, adding illogically: "After all, he is a murderer."

"How do you know?"

I stared at her, somewhat bewildered. "How do I know the visitor is a murderer?"

"No," she said. "How do you know he likes his beer cold?"

She betrayed not the slightest sign of alarm, not so much as the merest shudder. Either her failing hearing was worse than normal that day, or she was as happy to open the door to a self-confessed, convicted criminal as she was to her guardian angel. I surmised that Felisa was having one of those afternoons when her movie-obsessed mind was concentrated on just one thing: winning a few small bets from me with her celluloid riddles, as she liked to call them. I accepted the challenge to keep her happy, not without a certain depressing sensation that I was paving the way for my imminent transfer to a geriatric home.

"'Go home to your mother . . . tell her everything's alright and there aren't any more guns in the valley,'" she said in her croaking voice.

"Not now, Feli, please," I begged her.

"Five pesetas if you know who said that to a blond boy staring at him wide-eyed. Think about it, it's very easy."

"Some other time," I excused myself good-naturedly. "Didn't you hear what I said? I'm expecting a very special visitor."

"Yes, very special."

I looked at her askance as she pretended to be absorbed in sweeping again, head down. No doubt she was hatching some plot. I thought of my wife; she had always been right, insisting from day one that Felisa would never behave like a typical maid; by now she was too old and set in her ways to be brought into line. Besides, she always declared her spinsterhood and solitude were a militant act, even when a boyfriend appeared late in her life. He was called Señor Pàmias, a spruce, elderly gentleman with Fascist leanings who always complimented Felisa by saying she looked just like a beautiful actress of obscure Italian origin by the name of Irasema Dilián, who surfaced again in the stiff, purulent Spanish cinema of the Forties, and the secret sister (as Señor Pàmias whispered confidentially to her one distant day with a hint of passionate excitement) of Claretta Petacci, Benito Mussolini's ill-fated mistress. This fantasy seemed to me a surreal, erotic distillation of the Italianate Spanish Fascism in vogue during those years.

By then Felisa was well into her thirties and was still helping her widower father in a small shop on Calle Urgell which specialised in buying and selling old cinema photographs and posters, as well as all kinds of old magazines, novels based on films, postcards and flyers for collectors. She was usually to be found in a corner at the back of the shop, bent over the files of an incredible archive her father had begun in the days of silent cinema. Felisa claimed you could find everything in it, even the most abstruse, outlandish things such as the names of the supporting cast or the editor of the film version of *María Rosa*, the drama by the Catalan author Angel Guimerà shot in Hollywood in 1916 by Cecil B. DeMille. The fact was, as we shall see, that this constant daughterly devotion of hers to the archive was costing me quite a few pesetas. Her father's shop – he was the son of immigrants from Andalusia who came to Barcelona to work on the preparations for the 1889 Universal Exhibition and settled on the slopes of Montjuïc – was for many years an obligatory reference point for any film-loving collector. When he died, in 1947, Felisa kept the struggling business going another couple of years, then sold up and used the proceeds for a trip to Venice. On her return, she became a maid in the house of Señor Pàmias, who by now was married with children and lived in a villa with a garden in Horta. Years later, at Christmas 1964, she appeared at our home, sent by an employment agency my wife had been in touch with. She had good references, but never explained why she had quit overnight her job with her former admirer, Señor Pàmias. Pure Hollywood.

"You spend your whole day cooped up in here," Felisa said, still pretending to sweep. "That can't be good for you. You haven't been out since Carmen and the children left. And you should see how you look . . . Have you seen yourself in the mirror?"

"Felisa, be good to me, I've still got a lot of work to do . . ."

"I promised your wife I'd take care of you."

"That's fine, but I don't need a nurse or a surrogate wife, still less a mother-in-law."

"Aren't you going for a swim today?"

"It's not one of my days."

"You should go every day."

"For God's sake, have pity on me," I begged her with a laugh, "and simply be the beloved Felisa you have always been to the children and me, with more than fifteen years of impeccable service in this house."

"Hmm," she growled, then fell silent for a while before returning to the charge. "I've got another really easy one."

"I'm not up to riddles today, Felisa, really I'm not. And listen, don't go making jokes with the man I'm expecting."

"'Whoever you are, I have always relied on the kindness of strangers.' Who said that? I'm sure you remember. Who is that poor woman who declares herself to be so helpless, and in which film? Five seconds, and the bet's five pesetas."

I took a deep breath.

"Alright, but what have I told you? Have you understood what you need to do when this man arrives, or not?"

"Don't be angry, for heaven's sake. I only do it to distract you a little. You work too hard." She cleared her throat, then began coughing. "'The kindness of strangers.' And she lets herself be led away on the arm of that elderly gentleman. I cried when I saw that ending. Do you want a clue? Ten seconds."

She stroked her mysteriously youthful hair, still black as a raven's. The everlasting fringe on her forehead looked as though it had been painted on. Skilfully, she rolled the cigarette from one corner of her mouth to the other, all the while waiting with her sly, mocking smile for me to change my mind about joining in her game.

"O.K., you can have twenty seconds," she said, screwing up her eyes still further and allowing the cigarette smoke to curl up over her tiny, wrinkled, child's face. "Thirty seconds."

"No, I'm not playing."

Water off a duck's back. I had spent more than an hour blocked, staring at half a dozen pages scattered across my desk, pages smeared from top to bottom with handwritten comments. There were so many crossings out and corrections scrawled between the lines and in the margins that there was no more blank space, and, worse still, not the slightest doubt as to how useless all this effort was. Nor was there anything new about this calamitous spectacle. Empty words and smoke. I've spent half my life getting tangled up in writing drafts, and another half poking around in them, with no hope of things getting better with age or acquiring mastery of the trade. On the contrary, in recent years I've become even more keenly aware of my personal failure; I often feel as if I am dragging along the heavy weight of being a fraud and a lack of ability that I should at long last openly confess to. I can't explain why, but a moment always arrives when I am working on a book and I become disheartened, a moment when I feel like an impostor, a mask, a person disguised as a writer, someone who has usurped the authorship of that pile of tormented sheets of paper.

I concentrated my attention on a paragraph I had corrected many times, poking at the embers in search of a bit of warmth. While it was true that there was no trace of sentimentalism or any sign of personal melancholy or sickly-sweet pleadings, which in itself was quite encouraging, at the same time there didn't seem to be the slightest narrative tension. Simple sentences turned to ashes – that was all I had achieved after close to five hours' work. The form did not fit the content, and the words still insisted on not saying what they were supposed to say, especially in that snaking paragraph full of empty resonances that had as much chance of being worthy of being called literature as I had of winning the Nobel Prize for quantum physics.

"*Something terrible indeed,*" I read again, rescuing the second or third version buried beneath the crossings out, "*was obviously going on beneath those peroxide curls because, although the initial reaction of the passers-by was one of stupefaction and pity when they saw the woman lying prone on the tram rails, hands crossed over her chest and looking so defenceless, so at the mercy of her own delirium, the scene, now they could think it over more coolly, made them want to laugh out loud, because no-one in their right mind could have imagined anything so ridiculous, a more impossible and stupid way of being run over.*"

Let's see, I told myself, maybe if you briefly leave the reader in suspense: for example, adding some relevant observation about the suicidal woman's pink hands tranquilly folded across her chest, or seeing her bring her feet together in strict sepulchral symmetry, or closing her delicate eyelids ever so slowly, as they're touched by death's icy finger . . . but what part do I play in all this? Who do I identify with, where am I in this painstaking retelling of all this unedifying nonsense? Am I that boy with curly hair wearing espadrilles and a white shirt, the one we see from the back with a book under his arm, pushing his way through the crowd of neighbours and onlookers surrounding the woman lying on the rails, the one apparently glancing casually out of the corner of his eye at the inner thigh that the badly done-up housecoat allows a glimpse of? Well, it isn't easy to recognise oneself from behind, especially in the welter of other images linked to this extraordinary event that have persisted more strongly, such as the slightly thick, pinkish ankles contrasting with the grey cobbles, the porcelain skin that continues to emit its pale glow across time, the waxy eyelids closing on some pleasurable vision that leaves the lips half open because of the proximity, the brief touch or the pressure of another pair of lips, the breath of a long-desired kiss. And wasn't it here, glancing at the smudged lipstick on that mouth, the silk dagger on her thigh, and the crows still sniffing at the carrion and death at the foot of Mount Kilimanjaro, with the hyenas howling in the middle of the night, wasn't it here, with that first book under his arm and the battle in his blood between his heart and his manhood coursing through the veins, wasn't this when that boy felt a nostalgia for the future, the secret daydreaming that would mark his destiny, that other youthful passion that surpassed even what he felt when ogling Señora Mir's prone body or when her daughter Violeta allowed him to feel her breasts in a dark alleyway?

But the deception, the fraudulent nature of the words refused to go away. Throwing the biro down on the sheets of paper, I leaned back against the chair, my hands locked behind my head. The problem, I told myself, might perhaps lie in the discrepancy between the tame, sceptical man now attempting to bring that episode back to life, and the indomitable, intense youth who had lived it all those years earlier.

Then once again came the voice of Felisa, as if reaching me from the far side of the moon:

"'If I'd been a ranch, they would've named me Bar Nothing,'" she crooned in her most seductive tone. She had abandoned her sweeping and was staring at me. "It's said by a red-haired vamp who in real life was very unfortunate. Guess."

"I haven't the faintest idea."

"How can you have forgotten that dazzling toss of her head that eroticised a whole generation . . ."

"Please don't insist, have pity on me."

"You need to clear your mind a bit."

"What I need is a whisky with a splash of water."

"Normally by this time his highness has already gone for a swim or is flat out on the terrace with a book."

I forced myself to remain patient.

"Please, Felisa. Did you hear what I said?"

"The master will have his whisky in a moment. But first let's have that bet. Come on."

"I'm not betting anything with a cheat. You're just taking advantage of me."

I knew this wouldn't stop her. Sometimes at nightfall, with the first bats swooping round the terrace, the presence and guessing games of our beloved and indefatigable film buff could be a pleasant pastime, but they could also be a nightmare.

"'A ranch open to everyone,'" she insisted. "Shall I give you a clue? It takes place in Buenos Aires . . . No? How about this other one? 'I'm not interested in patriots. They carry their flag in one hand, while with the other they empty people's pockets.' It's said by a beautiful Swedish woman who's as healthy as an apple . . . Come on!"

Exhausted, all hope gone, I stretched my weary arms forward like a galley slave and bowed my head on the desk. But I didn't waste a second on her blasted riddle, because all of a sudden, in the bottom third of one of the most mutilated pages, in the middle of a six-lined paragraph that had become a jumble of crossed-out words, scrawled over and finally substituted, something had begun to stir and was calling out to me. Encouraged by arrows pointing to small blocks of notes in the margins, one of the rejected, trashed lines suddenly rose to its feet, slashed me with its black paw, then headed stiff and proud for the top of the page. Pushing its way in, it sat between the third and fourth lines and settled there, in the place that, on reflection, was its rightful home. At once, other sentences lost their earlier masks of deception and began to look in the right direction. Don't despair, you dummy, I told myself, all is not lost: beneath all those treacherous drafts there still breathes the dream of another life, more intense and truer than this one. There are no more forbidden topics or clandestine words, there's no need any longer to conceal them or replace them or say them under your breath. And so, after laying her head on the tram track, on that rusty, timeless iron bar half buried in the cobblestones of Calle Torrent de las Flors, the poor woman again folds her hands across her chest in an apparently devotional suicidal gesture and lies motionless, awaiting an impossible death . . .

Felisa's husky voice roused me from my thoughts:

"So then, I am to behave naturally when I open the front door to this gentleman." Stubbing out her cigarette in the ashtray on my desk, she cleared her throat and added: "Is that what you were trying to tell me?"

"More or less. But don't worry, we're not in any danger."

"Now I understand why your wife took the children and went so far away. So as not to have to receive a criminal in her own home."

Carmen had gone to Holland to visit her brother, whom she had not seen for twenty years. I'd have been happy to take a holiday there with her and the children, two months of doing nothing other than stroll through tulip fields and float along the canals of Amsterdam, but the blasted screenplay meant I had to stay in this noisy city with an elderly assassin for company and regular visits from unscrupulous movie nuts. None of this seemed to affect Felisa in the slightest.

"Doesn't that seem sacrifice enough to Madam Nosey-parker?"

"Yours truly couldn't say."

I decided it was time to stop joking and explain what was going on, in order to avoid any alarm or misunderstanding. I told her I'd been commissioned to write a film treatment based on a real event, a crime committed years earlier in a cinema in our own neighbourhood, and that I needed to do the research. What I didn't tell her was that it had been two weeks now and I hadn't really committed myself to the task, due to a lack of information and interest on my part, and because I preferred to work on my own writing.

"And seeing that the murderer is still alive . . ." I went on, then fell silent. All of a sudden, "murderer" seemed to me another of those words that emerge out of the darkness like a phantom, covered in dust and cobwebs and clearly robbed of all meaning. "Well, that's a manner of speaking . . . The fact is, the man I'm expecting has first-hand information on what happened, and he can advise me. So first-hand, Felisa," I said vengefully, measuring my words, "that he is in fact the author of that horrendous crime, in person. In flesh and blood, in other words. His name is Fermín Sicart, and he was the projectionist in the cinema booth where it all happened more than thirty years ago . . . Yes, don't pull that face. Who better to tell me what took place in there?"

And, I hastened to add, of course, there was no reason to be afraid, because the man had paid for his crime at the time. He had been put on trial soon afterwards, and he had served his sentence, so no doubt he was a changed man by now. Getting information directly from the murderer had been suggested by the film's producer, who years earlier had made contact with him for a different project that never got off the ground. He told me he was sure Señor Sicart would be pleased to talk to me if I paid him something – he had no idea how much – and he gave me his telephone number. I called Sicart at home; he was friendly and very willing to see me.

"So when he comes, try to act as naturally as possible," I warned Felisa. "Don't look suspiciously at him or anything, and above all don't hound him with questions. Just because a long time ago he was a projectionist doesn't mean he knows about films; he might not even like them. And I have to win his confidence, otherwise I'll be wasting my time and money."

Felisa took all this in with a slightly more rapid blinking of her eyes than usual, but wanted me to go into greater detail. I told her that for the moment I didn't know much more.

Did she remember the crime? She must do, it was the talk of Barcelona at the time.

"She was a poor prostitute, wasn't she?" Felisa said, her huge, sad eyelids drooping a little, as though fending off the memory. "Yes, it was horrible. Strangled with a length of film, wasn't she . . . Oh, ages ago."

I refreshed her memory. The crime had taken place in early January 1949. I had just turned sixteen, and I recall that for a long while it was the talk of the neighbourhood. Two friends of mine, kids from the same street, had been in the Delicias cinema that evening. They told me that, shortly before it all happened, the session was interrupted because the film had caught fire. They arrested the murderer straightaway; he was given thirty years, spent only a third of that in prison, and when he came out was able to make a new life for himself. Now Señor Sicart was a peaceful pensioner who played pétanque on Paseo de Sant Joan, close to my home. He lived alone in a modest boarding-house on Calle Indústria, and was in the habit of taking long walks.

As she listened, Felisa picked up the overflowing waste-paper basket and took the ashtray that only she had used from the desk.

"I see," she said. "Is that what you've been working on today?"

"More or less." I cast a sullen glance at the mistreated sheets of paper. "But there are too many things I don't yet know. I need to talk to Señor Sicart so he can clear them up."

"You're getting old," declared Felisa. "Well, I'll water the plants on the terrace before this . . . what's his name arrives. Do you need anything? Would you like a cup of tea?"

"No."

"With lemon?"

"No. Look, what did we agree, dear Felisa?"

"You had the chance to earn yourself another five pesetas, but you've lost it. A shame. Would you like sugar with it?"

"I don't want anything. I'll have a beer later with Señor Sicart."

"As you wish."

Pausing in the doorway before she left the room, Felisa turned to look at me, the wastepaper basket balanced on one hip and the ashtray and broom in her other hand. It was starting to grow dark, and the dim light still filtering in through the window cast a reddish glow on her roguish but affectionate features, where I also spotted a certain unease. I reflected that my wife had been right when she told me a fortnight earlier as she set off for Holland that Felisa would feel lonely without the children and the usual hustle and bustle around the house, so it might be a good idea for me to find her some extra tasks to do so that she would feel needed.

I am afraid that all I had managed to do was to instil fear in her. Maybe it's true that ever since the dictator's death words have taken on a different meaning, one I hadn't yet understood.

4

5. DELICIAS CINEMA. INTERIOR. DAY. FADE IN.

Like a diamond sparkling in the darkness, we see the beautiful singer and dancer with fiery hair seconds before her image freezes on the screen. First she almost completely loses her voice, and this sudden aphasia only serves to accentuate the lascivious temptation of her lips, glossy with lipstick, as they move suggestively, proffering heaven knows what delights, evoking disturbing emotions that have no need of words or music, as if drenched with a scandalous, furtive, decidedly obscene sexuality.

The first whistles and stamping of feet can be heard in the stalls. Two boys in the front row are stripping and devouring with their eyes the explosive star who is so suddenly mute. Her song can no longer be heard, but her body still writhes and provokes; bewitched and emboldened, the two boys feel their pricks stiffen between their legs, and go on listening and watching, open-mouthed: they haven't sneaked into the stalls of this sticky local cinema, at the risk of getting a slap across the ears from the usher, for a breakdown of the projector or a worn-out reel of film to frustrate them like this. Everything happens in a few seconds that seem an eternity. Even though the mouth is no longer singing, the lips are still moving silkily and provocatively, as if whispering a pure embodiment of sex, still offering feverish temptations.

But all of a sudden, at the point when the silent performance of this great beauty is at its most provocative, her smile at its most explicit, the swaying of her body sheathed in a black satin gown at its most suggestive, at the moment when she spreads her arms in a sweeping, passionate gesture of possession that envelops everyone in the casino and the cinema, an amorous embrace that in time will reach the furthest corners of the big wide world and cast a spell on future generations of devoted admirers, the moment when the body filmed in dazzling black-and-white has become pure sex beneath the spotlights, and just as, enticingly slowly, she peels the long glove from her arm and whirls it around in the air . . . at that very moment the image freezes and around her sensational mane of hair appears a timid constellation of grey and brown blotches, like a rash or small bubbles of a corrosive acid. The beautiful woman has still not had time to throw the glove to the expectant public in the casino, or the necklace she recklessly tears from her neck; she has just begun tantalisingly to pull down the zip on the side of her dress, but gets no further before her image is fixed and at the mercy of the celluloid gnawing away at her. At first they are random blotches, small butterflies of light that flutter here and there as if unable to make up their minds where to settle; some burst at once like soap bubbles, others spread and darken like ink blots, until the biggest, most active blotch quickly gains ground and begins to gobble up the other blotches and everything else it encounters: first the hair with its coppery reflections, lit by a dreamy light from behind her head, then the beautiful face, devouring the splendour of the smile and the gleaming eyes, then the silky shoulders, and finally the breasts, the swaying hips and the hand on the zip, the promise of a striptease.

Eventually the frozen image disappears completely, the lights in the hall go up, and there is a storm of whistles and protests from the audience.

CUT to the projection booth, the hands of the operator tugging at the snagged reel of film to make sure that the flame, if there is one, doesn't reach the drum. As usual, he is in such a rush he pulls out too much, and when he cuts the film he eliminates about a metre of images. He sits in front of the splicer, picks up the bottle of acetone and the brush. He has thrown the extra frames onto the floor – the black corkscrew of celluloid with its satiny length of film – and quickly starts to splice the reel. First he licks the gelatine off the film, then scrapes the edge with a razor blade and sticks the two ends together with acetone, blowing on it to speed up the process. Once this patching up is done, and before restarting the projector, he smiles towards a corner of the booth.

Sitting beside a pile of cans covered with a sack, a woman, naked but for a pair of black stockings and with a threadbare astrakhan coat round her shoulders, is nibbling on a roll while she watches the projectionist at work. She stands up, snaps the mauve garter against her snow-white thigh, and smiles as she approaches him.

CUT to the stalls of the cinema with the lights up and the screen blank. The whistling and stamping of the audience, most of them locals, grow even louder. One of the boys pokes his friend with his elbow and moans:

BOY 1: It's not fair! Just as she was about to strip!

BOY 2: Yes, damn it! She's already taken one glove off!

BOY 1: That's the censorship, *chaval*. They cut out the kisses, the legs, the arses and the tits. Christ! It makes me so mad! When the film comes back, what do you bet it won't show anything?

At last the lights go down and the protests subside. The film restarts at the moment when some casino employees grab hold of the provocative singer and force her off the dance floor. She is fully dressed, laughing outrageously, not in the least ashamed at what she has done.

The first boy pokes his companion in the ribs again.

BOY 1: See? Do you realise there's some film missing?

BOY 2: That's right! It's been cut! She was taking her dress off!

BOY 1: Exactly! Did you see how she was pulling down her zip?

BOY 2: Yes, I did!

BOY 1: Now watch what comes next. The guy gives the girl a slap worthy of a champion. Look! And do you know why? Because she behaved like a whore!

BOY 2: Yes? Do you think that's why, because she was stripping in front of everyone like a whore?

BOY 1: Like a prostitute. That's not the same as a whore. A whore is the lowest of the low, kid, almost as bad as a slut, which is the most disgusting of all . . .

BOY 2: So that's why he slaps her, because she's a prostitute?

BOY 1: Of course! Why else? We don't see it because they've cut that bit of the film, but she stripped off completely! That's why he slaps her about. It's as clear as day, *nano*.

FADE OUT TO BLACK

5

"He's here," Felisa said.

I could have sworn that when she heard the doorbell my assistant would have been startled, and would rush to open it with her heart in her mouth, complaining to herself as she dragged the broom along behind her, and that when for the first time in her life she found herself face to face with a murderer, she would take two or three steps back, not exactly out of fear, but from an automatic reaction produced by her own devious nature, her irrepressible urge to playact. And yet, when she announced Señor Fermín Sicart, I could tell from her eyes that she had not suffered or even pretended to suffer any shock. Instead, she seemed disappointed at having to carry out such a routine task, although she did as we had agreed: she ushered the visitor quickly through the living room out onto the terrace and left him standing there next to the balustrade, looking out over the city and the panorama of new roofs surrounding the C. E. Europa football club.

I hung back a moment to observe him through the French windows. I saw him turn and make his way with a bullfighter's swagger to the table and four metal chairs beneath the orange parasol, but he did not sit down. His arm jerked briefly as he smoked his cigarette, apparently lost in thought. I found it hard to believe that, as it appeared from his dossier and some photographs from the time, he had once been attractive to women. Our murderer was a man of around sixty, but he appeared much older; he was small and seedy-looking, but very stiff and erect, as if trying to claw a few centimetres out of the air with his head, a long neck that protruded from his drooping shoulders, his mouth a bitter line, and his dyed, jet-black hair combed back. He looked like a lottery ticket seller, his eyes hidden behind a pair of old-fashioned dark glasses with round metal frames, and his rigid body seemed more virile thanks to the raincoat draped round his shoulders. Some touches in the clothes he was wearing suggested an outmoded attempt to be stylish: the collar of his white shirt was raised at the back and turned down on the lapels of his charcoal-grey jacket. His trousers had turn-ups and a sharp crease, but ended too high above a pair of impeccable brown and white shoes. Overall, despite the dark glasses and his well-groomed appearance, he had a slightly comical, not in the least threatening, air. In fact, he looked like a relic from the sad, patched-up and spiv-like Spain of the post-war years, and it was only his insistent, stiff pose that suggested a hint of contained, or rather repressed, violence.

"There he is," Felisa said behind my back.

"Did you offer him a drink?"

"He doesn't want anything."

She took a packet of cigarettes out of her housecoat pocket, lit one and stood there staring at me, eyes narrowed behind the smoke. I waited to see if she was going to add anything, but she remained silent.

"Come on, don't play dumb, I'm sure he made some impression on you."

"Of course he did, looking like that, with those dark glasses and that raincoat from the year dot, on such a sweltering day. Did you get a good look at him? He's a damn psychopath."

"No, seriously: what's your impression of him?"

She shrugged.

"He looks like the man who deserved a better fate. He was poisoned, if you remember," she said, brusquely turning her back on me. "Think about it. I'll be in the kitchen."

I thought I knew what little man she was talking about – a distant shadow of the good noir movies of yesteryear, but I was sick and tired of her guessing games.

Two minutes later, I was shaking Fermín Sicart's hand and thanking him for his willingness to collaborate on something that must, I added by way of an apology, not be exactly pleasant for him. We sat down under the parasol, and I explained at some length what I wanted from him. I said I hoped that the amount of time that had passed would allow him to speak about that unfortunate event without feeling he was being in any way attacked.

"Don't worry about that," he cut in.

"In any case, allow me to insist on what I already told you on the telephone. If at any moment you feel awkward talking about anything, I'd like you to tell me straightaway . . ."

"No problem," he said with a slightly impatient gesture. "You ask the questions, and Fermín will answer."

When he spoke he barely moved his lips, and his gruff voice seemed to come from the pit of his stomach. I adopted my most persuasive tone and explained that I was not accustomed to this kind of task, that I had never gathered this sort of first-hand information in such a delicate, emotional matter. Emotional for him, of course.

"We'll have to go over episodes in your life you've probably tried hard to forget . . ."

"Ask away." He closed his fist on the table and cleared his throat. "Whatever you wish." He fell silent, smiled, cleared his throat again and added finally: "Lots of dough in this, isn't there?"

"What's that?"

"They have lots of dough. People in the movies."

"Ah, yes. I suppose they do. At least, some producers

have lots. But many films are made with grants. This one too, I'm sure."

He nodded without a word. I knew at once what was going through his mind. On the telephone the day before I had mentioned paying him something to compensate for his time, and now the moment had come for me to ask him if he had any definite figure in mind. When I did so, he merely shrugged in an offhand way, but I would have loved to see his eyes behind the dark glasses. After a few seconds, he said:

"Whatever you think is fair."

"It won't take us long. One week will be enough, two at most . . ." I thought: It depends on what you're willing to tell me, but what I said was: "It will depend on me organising myself properly. And on your memory, of course. Well, I'd thought of offering you 5,000 pesetas. Does that seem fair?"

For the first time, I saw a faint smile appear on his thin lips.

"For a week's work?"

"It could be two." I hastened to add: "In which case I'll pay you double, of course. Are you free in the afternoons?"

"All afternoon?"

"I'm not sure . . . Let's say two or three hours. As you like, in your own time. Whenever you grow tired, or feel it's too much, we can stop and leave it for another day."

He agreed pensively, stroking an earlobe.

"For a week . . . Why don't we round the number up and call it six thousand?"

His figure didn't round anything up, and seemed to me excessive. I could make out his searching eyes behind the glasses, awaiting my reply.

"That's fine."

"Fantastic." He seemed to relax, said nothing for a while, but then asked brightly: "Tell me, who's going to do the film?"

"Oh, a very prestigious director."

"No, I mean who will play my part."

"Ah, they haven't cast the actors yet. It's too soon for that. Are you thinking of anyone in particular?"

"No, not at all. Ever since I came out of prison, almost twenty-five years ago, I can only have been to the cinema half a dozen times. Before, I used to be up-to-date with things, but not now." He crossed and uncrossed his legs with studied care, then added, as if the answer was of no great importance to him: "And this film director, you say he's good?"

"Oh yes, really good." I took a deep breath, just as I often do when I hold on to the side of the pool before turning and plunging back into the water for another length: more to get some oxygen into my brain than into my lungs. Although to be honest, swimming seems to me much less tiring and boring than having to define Héctor Roldán's talent. Maybe that was why, exacting personal vengeance, I said: "In his day, the director was a real emblem of militant anti-Francoism, and he still is. Even so, if it's art we're talking about, a single shot by Raoul Walsh, to name someone who made action movies, is worth more than all the films he has made."

Sicart did not so much as blink. I named a couple of Héctor Roldán's pictures, and he thought he had a vague recollection of them, but they were from the years he spent in prison and he did not think he had seen them. He expressed himself well, speaking succinctly and directly. He confessed he hadn't read any of my novels and was not so stupid as to apologise for it. Impassive, wary but polite, sitting ramrod straight on the chair, he still had the raincoat carefully draped round his shoulders. It dawned on me that all his gestures were nothing more than poses, the fantasy overload or perfume of a dormant threat that, in spite of all the years that had passed since the crime, he imagined he was still capable of transmitting: a nod to his own personal mythology, a sort of self-homage to his shadowy past from which he couldn't or didn't want to free himself. I decided to go gently, and so began by asking him about his job as a film projectionist. He had very precise memories about his profession.

"Nowadays it's all very modernised, but back then you needed a proper apprenticeship," he said with deliberate disdain. "Now the whole film is in a single box and the machine does everything. All you have to do is press a button. Back then, you had to change the reel every twenty minutes, because that was the length of each can of film, and there were two projectors, so that when you went to change from one to the other you had to be very careful if you didn't want to miss any part of the film and hear the audience protest . . . I don't mean to boast, but I was one of the best at making sure the reels followed on smoothly, I lost very few frames. And another important thing: in those days, the films were made of nitrate, and that was highly flammable. Do you know what we did if any of them caught fire?"

"An extinguisher, I suppose."

"No, sir. A soda siphon."

"Really? I don't believe you."

"Yes, really. The arc lamps gave off sparks, and if there was any sign of a flame: zap it with the siphon! I kept two in the projection booth and always tested them before a screening. Yes, sir, there were always a couple of soda siphons next to the projectors. I'm talking about local cinemas, of course. And in the cupboard we used to have a wet blanket to stifle any possible outbreak of fire."

"Gosh, that's very interesting."

"The thing is, there was real danger. Especially if you had female company . . ." He smiled, inviting my complicity. "If you follow me."

"Oh, of course." I stirred in my seat. "Look, before we get on to the main question, which is to say, what happened in the Delicias cinema that eleventh of January, I'd like to clear up a few things about that woman . . ."

"You mean Carol?"

"Yes, Carolina Bruil Latorre. I need to know about her life before she became a prostitute. We know she performed in several variety revues, and that she was a police informant. You stated that you had nothing against her, and that you had seen her for the first time that fateful day . . ."

"I lied," he said curtly.

"Oh, you don't say. Why did you lie?"

"Well, the fact is, I don't know. I suppose I thought it was the right thing to say."

"But why?"

"To protect her. She may have been a whore, but I liked her a lot, you know."

"When did you meet? Where?"

"In Panam's, a bar with hostesses on the Rambla. That was a long while before any of this happened. I seem to remember it was in 1947. Another girl on the game, Encarnita, introduced me to her. But that day I hardly even noticed her. Carol had a regular pimp. A member of the Falange, a real braggart who loved to show off, a lowlife."

"I know. We'll talk about that later. Panam's was a place for call girls, and you used to telephone there when you wanted female company. Even when you were working, is that right?"

"Well, that was where Encarnita, a blind whore who lived on my street, used to work."

"Did you say blind?"

"In those days she could still see a little. She ended up completely blind, but she dealt with it very well. Seriously. She used to do it by touch, feeling her way . . . and she was very popular, believe me."

"Really?"

"She had a way of touching you that . . . well!" He smiled, and pushed the glasses up his nose with his middle finger. "A real treat. She had been a masseuse. My mother said her hands had healing powers, or something of the sort."

"You don't say!"

"My mother was very fond of her. Encarnita was like one of the family. She used to come round when she was a little girl . . ."

"So let's see. You used to invite those prostitutes to the cinema, then have a snack or supper with them up in the booth, is that it?"

"From time to time. If they didn't have another job, obviously."

"When was the first time you called Lina to the Delicias?"

"Lina? Oh yes, but I called her Carol. She was also known as the Cat or the Chinese Girl. That was her artistic name from the days when she worked in variety." He gave what sounded like a guttural laugh, bowed his head, and said nothing for a while. "Let me think . . . Yes, the first time was one evening when Encarnita had agreed to come to the Delicias to have a bite with me, in other words . . . well, you know what I mean.

But that day Encarnita was ill, or had another client, I can't remember. The thing is, she sent Carol in her place."

"And from then on, how often?"

"In the cinema, or elsewhere? Because after that, we saw each other a lot, almost always in Panam's . . ."

"No, I mean in the projection booth."

"You know, I really liked Carol. She was easy to get on with. Her only weakness was that she drank a lot, she drank like a fish . . ."

"Right. How often?"

"Oh, that's funny!" He gave a throaty laugh. "That's the damned question the nosey priest used to ask us in the confessional when we were kids!"

"But it's not the same, is it?" I said, laughing with him.

"Of course not! Let's see . . . I've no idea how often. I'd say three or four times."

"No more than that? Between '47 and '49, when it all ended, two years elapsed. You say you liked her a lot, that you even came to love her, but over those two years you only used her services three or four times?"

For an instant he looked perplexed.

"No, it must have been more. You see, Carol was one of those classy whores who can steal your heart . . . I don't know if you follow me. Although you might not believe it, she really was lovable."

"Do you mean you fell in love with her?"

"Well yes, I think I did," Sicart admitted. "Do you know what was best about her? Well, I won't say . . . She was a very affectionate sort. There was something Oriental about her, she had the eyes of a beautiful Chinese woman. I don't know how to explain it. Like a quiet, clever little Chinese woman, who knew everything, if you get me? The thing is, she had worked in the theatre, like her husband; she had been a dancer in revues on Avenida Paralelo, and in variety shows. Yes, I felt good with her . . . She was a woman who listened to you and didn't pester you, one of those who while you're doing it with her let's you go on thinking about your own things, if you follow me . . . She would have made a good wife."

I remained silent for a few seconds. Then I commented:

"But you said you didn't see her very often."

"Yes, I'm sorry, I said three or four times, but it must have been more. The thing is, when I fucked my Carol, I mean really fucked her, with all my heart and soul, not just with . . . well, you know, I won't say it . . . I mean, I've only fucked like that two or three times in my whole life, and then you know what happens, you remember those two or three occasions above all, because they were out of this world, unforgettable, like between two lovers. What can you do, that's the lousy reality . . ."

"That's fine. I understand you."

"You'll have to forgive me, sometimes I can't express myself properly."

"You explain yourself perfectly. Well anyway, was it always in your booth at the Delicias?"

"Almost always."

"It doesn't seem like a very suitable place for . . ."

"Perhaps not, for how you imagine it. But you have to put yourself in my place," he said, with complete conviction. "It's all about getting used to something in this life, don't you think? I learnt to fuck in Calle Las Tàpies, standing up against a wall . . . and that's no joke. But it wasn't like that, of course. In the projection room you're glad of the company, especially in winter. They were friends of mine. Back then I lived in the Chinese quarter, on Calle Sant Ramon, and there were two girls who were streetwalkers who lived near us. We'd known each other since we were kids, we'd been brought up together. I don't know if this makes sense, but some days when they didn't have many clients and were bored, I'd ask them up to the booth for something to eat. The noise of the projector used to bother them, but I was used to it. And don't go thinking it was all just for a fuck, that wasn't always why we got together . . . Though I have to admit that in those days I was full of life, at twenty-five you charge at everything, don't you? I don't know if you follow me."

"Fine. I was wondering where your colleague went while you and she were . . ." – I was about to say "having sex" but managed to stop myself in time – ". . . were busy. Because you didn't work alone, did you?"

"No, there were two of us. But you see, in those days a good operator could manage on his own, if need be. And I was one of the good ones, though I say so myself."

It didn't escape my attention that he had corrected me: those in the profession don't say projectionist, but operator.

"I'd been Señor Augé's assistant," he said. "In the union they called him Germán, but his name was Liberto Augé. He taught me the job, he was in charge of things for many years, but by the time we were assigned to the Delicias cinema he was already on his uppers, he had problems with his eyesight and often had to give up before the film ended. So I learned to manage on my own."

"Did Señor Augé approve of you inviting prostitutes to the projection booth?"

"No way! He used to say to me: 'Kid, those sluts will only cause you problems . . .'" All of a sudden Sicart lowered his head and adjusted his dark glasses, as if to make sure I couldn't see his eyes. "He was a good man. He was losing his sight because he had diabetes, and had problems focusing the films. He got really upset when he heard the audience protesting. Normally, when I saw he was in a bad way, I let him change the first two reels and then sent him down to talk to the woman in the box office, or to have a coffee with a splash of brandy in the bar on the corner . . . That was all I could do for him." He fell silent for a while, lost in thought. "He had a dog called Sparky that he was really fond of. He was a good man."

"It sounds like you were really fond of him," I said. "Or am I wrong?"

"He was a great chief operator. The best. He taught me all I know."

"Did Augé know Carolina Bruil? Did he have much to do with her?"

"He only saw her two or three times."

"Good. We can talk about Liberto Augé in due course . . . Would you like a beer, a soft drink?"

"Do you have any wine?"

Felisa brought a bottle of Rioja with two glasses on a tray. By then, Sicart had taken off his sunglasses and was wiping them with a handkerchief. As he did so, I got a good view of wrinkled tortoise eyelids over grey, lifeless eyes. Felisa didn't come out with any awkward comment or look warily at him, but took longer than necessary to serve us. She got in ahead of me to uncork the bottle, and opened it so close to Sicart's face and with such violence that she almost took his nose off with her elbow. Sicart managed to dodge the blow and sat considering her with amused curiosity.

"Watch what you're doing, señora!"

"Thank you, Felisa, I'll pour." I was afraid something might happen, and swiftly took the bottle out of her hands. Too late: Felisa glanced at my guest, then at me, stood there with the tray under her arm, and cleared her throat three times.

"Do you recall that yesterday I couldn't think how that

scorpion story went? Well, I've remembered now. It's like this: a scorpion wanted to cross a river, so he asked a frog to carry him on his back . . ."

"Not now, Felisa, later . . ."

"Later I have things to do." She gave me a crestfallen look and shrugged. "Suit yourself . . ."

"I'll call if we need anything," I told her. As Felisa withdrew, grumbling to herself, I filled our glasses and smiled apologetically at Sicart. "Don't worry, she's harmless. She's been here so long she's like one of the family."

Sicart raised his glass and blew out his cheeks.

"Goodness! What a way she has with a corkscrew!"

"Let me repeat that if at any point you feel uncomfortable . . ."

"Don't worry about that."

This was evidently his favourite expression, which on this occasion was delivered with a hint of impatience. At any rate, although my main objective was to learn about the crime, I had no intention of asking him straight off to tell me how he did it, when he decided to do it, or what state of mind he was in at the time. First of all, I wanted to establish a sense of mutual trust. I preferred to approach the subject by asking different questions, showing my interest in secondary figures, and gradually build up to the climax. For example: after leaving prison, did he return to his job as a film operator?

"No. I worked for a couple of years in a waste disposal factory in Badalona. After that I went into partnership with a fellow from Mallorca who lived in the Ribera neighbourhood. He had a hair business."

"A hair business?"

"Hairpieces: wigs and toupés. We did quite well. You'd be surprised how many men and women wear hair that isn't theirs."

"I see." I tried to steer the conversation back to what interested me. "Tell me something. Why do you think the Politico-Social Brigade got involved in a case that had more to do with the murder squad?"

"I don't know. There were some very odd things about it all. They said I could have acted on behalf of someone who wanted Carol silenced forever, because she was a whore who knew too much . . . Things like that. That she had been a police informant, and that she ended up paying for it . . . All lies."

"What can you tell me about her pimp, the one called Ramón Mir?"

"I've already told you. He was a loudmouthed Falangist. His hair was always slicked back with lots of brilliantine. They said he was a nutcase."

"Did you have much to do with him?"

"We bumped into each other in Panam's a few times. I didn't want anything to do with him."

"At the end of '47, when you met Carolina, she had been with that fellow for two years. And she stayed with him. Didn't you mind that? Weren't you jealous?"

"Not at first. Let's see: Carol was a prostitute, why deny it? And she felt very vulnerable: she needed protection. I couldn't have cared less that her pimp was a Falangist, but it suited her. Later on I learnt he was a lowlife as well, that he forced her to attend parties he organised for high-ups in the Falange or the Civil Government, I don't remember which, who were friends of his . . . She told me so herself."

He added that this was what he had said when he was interrogated by the police, the examining magistrate, and also when he had had to undergo a psychiatric test, but warned me I shouldn't waste time looking for any of this in the dossier, because I wouldn't find a single reference to it. The police investigation into Carolina Bruil's career as a prostitute made no mention of it, nor would I find any trace of it in the court proceedings.

"Goodness, that sounds interesting."

I told him that I needed all possible information about his work in the Delicias cinema: how a projector in a cinema with continual performances had been operated thirty or forty years earlier, and what they had to do when the reel snapped. Also, what he used to do when the projection was going smoothly and didn't need much attention. What he did when he was on his own, etc.

"Maybe, if we start there, it will be easier for you to explain . . ."

"Well actually, I'm not sure about that," he said. "I'm afraid

I won't be much use to you about what interests you most."

"I don't understand."

He took another sip of wine and sat thinking for a few seconds.

"Perhaps I should have made it clear before we started. Let's see . . ."

He uncrossed his legs, then crossed them again with an elegant flick. He took a silver-plated cigarette case out of his inside jacket pocket and offered me one. How many years had it been since I saw someone using a cigarette case? The last time must have been in some film or other. I took an American cigarette; he did the same, pulled out a lighter and lit both cigarettes. He didn't put the case away but sat twiddling it between his fingers. After blowing the smoke slowly out of his mouth, he added thoughtfully:

"You've read everything related to the trial, haven't you?"

"Yes, and several police files."

"Then you'll know that shortly after I was arrested, I suffered a serious mental breakdown."

"In the report it states that you suffered from speech disorders and problems with your vision, so your first confession must to some extent be of questionable value . . ."

"Well, look, I couldn't get the horror of what I'd done out of my mind . . ." He sat there blankly, and for a moment I thought I had lost him. "That blood-stained length of film round her beautiful neck . . . Sorry for mentioning that . . .

Even now I've no idea . . . I'm sorry."

"That's alright. We can talk about something else if you prefer."

"No. I know . . . the thing is, afterwards I tried five times to kill myself . . . five, no less," he repeated (I remembered that in the trial records it said he had only tried to do so twice, but I didn't want to interrupt him), "which meant the doctors put me through such an aggressive therapy that for quite a while I even forgot my own name. But you already know all that, don't you?"

"More or less. I know you were interned in the psychiatric centre at Ciempozuelos. Tell me about this aggressive therapy."

"They called that nonsense 'shock therapy'. Lots of talk and lots of medication. They gave me . . . what's it called? A brainwashing. For three months they kept on asking me to tell them what had happened, then silence and daily doses of forgetting in the shape of pink pills, they stuffed me full of them – I had pink pills coming out of my ears . . ."

"I see. And who ordered the erasing of your memory as therapy?"

Sicart picked his glass up again, and raised it in a toast.

"Dr Tejero-Cámara, a military doctor with the rank of colonel. He was the head of a research team into some damned kind of study related to that, to the ability to forget. The sly old fox was an eminence in his field, apparently. There was a wall full of diplomas in his consulting room, and photographs of him with the Caudillo and Doña Carmen. He was held in high esteem, and was a psychology professor at a university . . ."

"I know who he was."

"He studied my case and decided I was a degenerate who had drunk anarchist ideas at my mother's breast, a mental defective with an Iberian Anarchist Federation credential. He used his own curative method, which they said he had begun to put into practice with Republican prisoners during the Civil War. Apparently he emptied their brains, scooped out all the Bolshevik ideas – the ones that had led them to Marxism or anarchism, the . . . what did he call it? The Red gene." He nodded thoughtfully. "Me an anarchist, and with the Red gene! Unbelievable, even as a joke. What they did was inject me with senile dementia, the sickness old people get."

I looked him in the eye. He was still flipping the cigarette case between his fingers.

"It's no laughing matter!" he repeated. "The Red gene! That must be really shit! He really had it in for Catalan anarcho-syndicalists, the bastard . . ."

"Did you confess to being an anarcho-syndicalist?"

"No, of course not, but the medical team diagnosed me as that! So I had to go through a process of 'depersonalisation' – that's what they called it, which was similar to being demented . . . Well, they did relieve me of the tremendous weight of the past, I'll give them that. Which on reflection is a good thing, isn't it? At least, as far as I can tell . . ."

I had read dreadful things about the practices of that particular military doctor, abusive therapies that a good many Republican prisoners had been subjected to. I'd even read about the famous Red gene, but I thought that by 1949, the year Sicart was sent to the Ciempozuelos centre, they had stopped being applied. Although I didn't entirely dismiss the idea of an induced amnesia, justified or not by the mental state of a patient on the brink of suicide, I also considered that Sicart might be suffering from a congenital mental illness, an age-related deterioration of his faculties – what shortly afterwards became known as Alzheimer's disease. Of course, that only complicated things still further.

"Your psychiatric report was signed by someone called Dr Suárez y Gil, who died three years ago," I told him. "And Dr Tejero-Cámara died more than twenty years ago. I'd have liked to talk to them. Because you see, if I'm truthful with you . . ." I paused and watched him drain his glass of wine, "your version has several very grey areas."

"Do you think so?"

"Well, I find it hard to believe in the amnesia you were finally diagnosed with. I'm no expert, but as a solution to the problem of memory loss – I'm not sure, but it sounds to me like an excuse."

I waited for him to say something, and when he didn't, I went on:

"Did any neurosurgeon do anything to you?"

"What do you mean, 'do anything'?"

"If they touched your head. An operation."

"You mean . . .?"

"Yes. A lobotomy."

"Oh, that! No, sir. I may not have much brain, but it's intact." He smiled broadly, furrowing his brow. "No, don't worry. I've studied the matter, and know that people who've suffered a lobotomy are unable to learn anything new but have a very good memory of what they lived through before the operation . . . No, Dr Tejero-Cámara had other methods. He would say to me: 'Sicart, don't cultivate memory, it's a poisonous bloom. We all have things that happened to us that are best forgotten.' And it's true, there are certain things it's best not to keep in your memory, aren't there?"

He was still fiddling with the cigarette case.

"Yes, possibly. Alright, let's talk about the famous uncontrollable impulse. In your medical records it states that this impulse was responsible for what you did, the cause that would explain what happened. Don't you think that's a bit odd?"

"I don't know what to say."

I studied him in silence for a few seconds.

"Do you know something? Nowadays a lot of people say the past should be left untouched. Sacrosanct. What do you think?"

He shrugged, still holding the case in his hands.

"It's all the same to me. But I think everyone has the

right to forget certain things, don't they?"

"Of course. The question is whether the things you want to forget belong exclusively to you, or are shared with other people. And I'm not referring to forgetting so much as to the erasure of memory."

"What do you mean? Aren't they the same?"

"No. Forgetting can be involuntary. The erasure of memory, especially in this country, is usually a well-planned strategy. But let's leave that there. Don't think it doesn't interest me, though. We'll come back to it later."

"You're in charge."

"Tell me a bit about Carolina Bruil. How do you remember her?"

"Goodness. Right now?"

"Let's see what you can tell me. I'll leave it up to you."

"I wouldn't know where to begin." He seemed all of a sudden very confused. "I prefer that you ask me questions."

He sat for a while head down, as if expecting a blow from on high.

"I wonder why she said 'Hurry up' just before."

"Me too. And if I'm honest, I prefer not to know why she said it."

"Well, it doesn't matter. There's time." I reached for the bottle of wine. "Would you like another glass?" He nodded and I poured it. "There are lots of other things I need to know. For example, what was the place like where everything occurred? I mean the projection booth at the Delicias cinema. How would you describe it?"

"Oh, a mousehole." He raised his head, pushed his glasses further up his nose with a flick of his index finger, took a sip of wine without letting go of the cigarette case, and added, smiling faintly: "Let me see . . . There was a table, two chairs, the cupboard for the reels, the clock, a water jug, a coat stand, a first aid cabinet, two soda siphons . . . As you see, we had everything. And on the table there was always a bottle of acetone, a paintbrush, scissors, razor blades, the splicer and a pair of white gloves . . . everything we needed for our work. Señor Augé also had a little electric oven to heat up his supper and a cage with a budgerigar in it. I still don't know how that bird managed to put up with the noise from the projector. Carol didn't like to see the poor thing shut in like that, she kept saying we should let it go. Whenever she came, I would cover the cage with a cloth . . . But do you know what Fermín can't forget, what poor Fermín can still see clearly, and sometimes, to be frank, even with tears in his eyes . . . ?"

I didn't know what to say.

"The two soda siphons?" I suggested.

"Carol's thighs, if you will forgive me saying so. Her warm thighs round my neck. Yes, sir; you can't imagine how affectionate a whore can be. Ah, my poor, beloved, unfortunate Carol!" The case was still spinning in his hands. "Although, believe me, she had her little ways . . . Do you know what she used to do? She would take the strips of film that I had hanging up with clips and those on the floor, and examine them closely against the light. If she saw any actress she thought was beautiful, she would climb on a chair and throw the strips out of the skylight that gave onto the street below. They're for my boys, she would say. And on the pavement outside, the youngsters fought to see who would get them . . ."

He stood up, shaking his head sadly. I decided to observe him without saying anything. He stood there, peering down at the cigarette case as if seeing it for the first time, as if it were something that didn't belong to him, and which left him bemused. All of a sudden, with an almost violent gesture, he stretched out his arm and offered the case to me, apologetically. "I'm sorry. Oh, I hope you didn't think I was going to pinch it."

I reacted slowly and awkwardly. With an unconscious reflex action, I held my hand out and took the cigarette case.

"No, of course not. Why would I think such a thing if it's yours anyway?" Then I said with a smile: "Or should I see it as a gift from you?"

He looked startled, stared at the case in my hand, looked at me, and then again at the case. He snatched it back, returning my smile.

"Nooo!" Putting it into his pocket, he added, with a forced laugh: "Christ! You'll be thinking to yourself what strange tricks that Fermín plays, won't you? Well, I'm off now. When do we start?"

"How about Tuesday next week? I have some things to do before then, and I need to gather more information. Shall we say at five in the afternoon?"

"That's fine. Whatever you say."

6 6 6

7. BOOTH AT DELICIAS CINEMA. DAY.

The whir of the projector drowns out the film soundtrack. In the darkness behind the machines, Sicart is sitting beside the splicer at the table, making himself a roll to eat. He cuts a slice of bread on a piece of newspaper, opens a tin of anchovies and pours himself wine from a bottle.

SICART: A drop of wine, Señor Augé?

Standing beside the projector as he checks a reel, Augé wipes his hands on a cloth and narrows his eyes so that he can see Sicart properly.

AUGÉ: Not now. I have . . .

As if stunned by the noise of the projector, Augé shakes his head and gropes for somewhere to steady his trembling hand. From the auditorium comes the sound of people stamping and a voice shouting "Focus!" Clumsily, obviously finding it hard to train his eyes on the machine and control his trembling hands, Augé recovers and moves to correct the focus, but without success.

Sicart sees this and quickly goes to help. He gently edges his colleague aside and attends to the problem.

SICART: Don't worry. Let me do it.

He adjusts the lens, and the stamping and shouted protests subside in the auditorium. Sicart peers through the little front window to make sure everything has calmed down, then turns his attention to the chief operator, who appears confused and dejected.

AUGÉ: Dammit! I've got those blasted cobwebs in my eyes again . . .

SICART: Don't you feel well? Come and sit down.

Taking him by the arm, he helps him sit at the table. Augé rubs his eyes.

AUGÉ: You need to pay attention: there are still two reels left. I'm fine, don't worry, it'll soon pass . . .

SICART: No, you're not fine. You'd better go out for a while and get some fresh air. Go to the bar on the corner and have a coffee with brandy.

AUGÉ (*struggling to his feet*): You're expecting company, you rascal, that's why you want me out of here. Don't think I was born yesterday. Be careful, those whores are going to give you something nasty.

Feeling his way, he allows Sicart to lead him to the door.

SICART: Have a chat with Matilde down below in the box

office. Or go home. Tomorrow's another day. There's not much left to do here, and I can cope on my own.

Augé, head bowed and disconsolate, pauses in the doorway and looks back fondly at his assistant. He pats Sicart's cheek.

AUGÉ: Don't forget to use gloves if you have to splice something. And be very careful . . . And I don't just mean about your job, because I know you're pretty good at that. I mean those sluts who steal your dough.

SICART: Don't say that, because it's not true. I've already told you, they're honest girls. Go on, go home. And take care of yourself, Señor Augé. You're not so young anymore.

8. PANAM'S CLUB. SEMI-DARKNESS. INTERIOR. DAY.

The Panam's Club towards the end of September 1947, as we see from a calendar hanging up behind the bar. The sound of dice being shaken in a cup and soft dance music playing as a travelling shot shows the dimly lit staircase; at the bottom on the right an old woman with gypsy features selling cigarettes and matches is dozing on a folding chair. The travelling shot takes in the length of the bar, which is attended by a short barman with a wooden expression. He is rolling the dice opposite a fat customer with an easy grin perched on a high stool, cigar in mouth and clutching a brandy glass. Seated at a table next to the dance floor, Carol (we will use her real name, as her screen name has not yet been decided) and her friend Encarnita are chatting, looking bored as they wait for clients. The other tables are empty, and so is the dance floor. It's early evening. Carol applies lipstick, while Encarnita is drinking redcurrant juice from a tall glass, then gropes for the cigarette lighter on the table and lights a menthol cigarette.

ENCARNITA: Tell me something, Carol. Why do they call you the Cat? Who gave you that nickname?

CAROL (*with a sad smile*): That was my stage name, when I used to work in the theatre. I was Chen-Li, Puss in Boots.

ENCARNITA: My mother told me she saw you once in a revue at the Selecto cinema. You worked with your husband, didn't you?

CAROL: He wasn't my husband. Or the father of my son, as some people thought. And he didn't work with me. I used to dance on my own, with my legs covered in glitter paint . . . my mask and red boots . . . I was stunning! He did proper theatre, even if it was amateur. He could have been a good character actor, he had talent, and the looks of a matinée idol. But he had no luck.

Her voice gradually fades, and eventually she falls silent, as if it pains her to remember. Encarnita gazes at her affectionately and feels for her friend's hand. When she finds it, she gives it a squeeze. Carol pushes the ashtray towards her, but Encarnita misses it with her ash.

CAROL: What are you waiting for to use glasses, dearie? Or is your heart still set on a guide dog?

ENCARNITA: Yes, darling. A sweet guide dog, a Labrador!

At that moment the Falangist Ramón Mir Altamirano comes striding rather unsteadily into the Panam's Club. He is wearing a black leather jacket and a blue shirt. Pale-complexioned, with a jutting chin, black hair smoothed back, and a pencil moustache above a scowling mouth. He has drunk several too many, and looks quite ill, even though he keeps up his air of bravado. Shaking his wet clothing, he mutters something like "It's pouring out there, and it's damned cold!" As he passes Carol he stops for a moment to stroke her neck, or rather to squeeze it in a clumsily possessive gesture. She murmurs a contemptuous greeting and makes to stand up, but Mir keeps her seated by pressing down on her shoulder. He staggers over to the bar, where he confronts the barman as he is rolling the dice.

MIR: I want the ugliest whore in here, Paco.

BARMAN (*as wooden-faced as ever*): You won't find any ugly ones in here, comrade.

MIR (*smiling at Carol*): Well, one with tiny tits, then.

BARMAN (*to the fat client*): It takes all sorts, doesn't it? (*To Mir*) Look, for your information we only get good-looking, well-educated people in here.

MIR: Alright then, one who has a squint, or false teeth, or a face full of spots! I'll make do with that. *(He chortles and slaps the fat client's back)* And have her dress up in drag! Ha ha ha!

FAT CLIENT: Look, friend, why don't you go and sleep it off somewhere else?

MIR (*confronting him, arms akimbo*): Who the hell asked you? Let me see, you there, yes you! Your papers.

FAT CLIENT: That's enough, comrade, don't make a fuss!

MIR: Family name and first name! Quick about it!

FAT CLIENT: For heaven's sake, what's got into you?

MIR: Shut up and answer my question. Are you Spanish?

FAT CLIENT: Me? . . . On the contrary.

MIR (*taken aback*): What do you mean by that? Are you Catalan?

FAT CLIENT: No, sir. I was born sterile.

MIR (*forcefully*): So you think this is a joke, do you? Do you know what you are? I'll tell you straight out, the way we military men like to talk: You're an idiot! A jackass! Come on, your papers!

N.B.: This is Ramón Mir Altamirano – a real person who will be given a pseudonym, as will Fermín Sicart and Carolina Bruil Latorre – a supporting character who I think could end up playing an important role in the plot, or whatever takes the place of the plot. A loony Falangist, long past the days of his heroic campaign liquidating Bolsheviks shoulder-to-shoulder with the Nazis, all his ammunition and war cries long since spent, his imagined youthful guard duties and dreams floating away with his starry comrades, he has embarked on a drunken decline towards an unhappy end. He has already abused the influence of his blue shirt, already marched and sung and strutted his glory days, taken advantage of the patriotic-religious pomp and ceremony as often as necessary, already denounced all the suspected Reds and hostile elements in his neighbourhood, already thrown his weight around, slandered, and laid his hands on as much as he can, already turned his lover into a prostitute and police informant, caroused and quaffed all he can thanks to the victors' camaraderie and privileges, and now is beginning to display signs of a madness and confusion that will eventually lead to him losing his position as a city councillor and the authority he still wields thanks to his leather military belts and big pistol, the yoke and arrows and the red-embroidered shield he wears over his heart, which in its turn is about to tell him it has had enough. In this part of the narrative we do not yet know much about this braggart, but I don't think that matters.

Anyway, suddenly the telephone in Panam's rings. It's Fermín Sicart in the Delicias cinema. When it rings at one end of the bar, Encarnita is talking to a client at the opposite end. He is busy fondling her backside. The two of them laugh. The barman takes the call and gestures to Encarnita. She gropes her way to the telephone and takes Fermín's message: he says he is expecting her as agreed, and tells her to hurry up because the churros and coffee are growing cold. "Don't expect me today, my love," Encarnita replies, "I can't come this evening." As she makes her excuses, she looks over at Carol sitting on her own at their table, drinking a glass of brandy. Encarnita says: "If you like I can send my friend Carol.

I've told you about her, she's better than me and a great girl, you'll like her. But you'll have to give her more than a milky coffee and churros, she's having a hard time, with a stack of problems."

The client calls her back, and Encarnita hangs up and hurries over to him. She bumps into him and laughs, squinting as she strokes and caresses him. She asks him to wait a minute, then turns towards Carol and suggests she go to the cinema in her place. She will have a great time, she says. "Fermín is a funny, affectionate sort. He always pays well, and the job includes a snack and supper too sometimes, and if you want you can watch the film." Carol replies that she isn't in the mood for company today, she's tired and sad. But Mir, who's been listening in to their conversation, tells her she should go because she has nothing better to do, and shows a sudden interest in this client who is offering food. "Is he the projectionist at the Delicias cinema, where that fellow Augé works?" Encarnita says that's right and then, fearing what the belligerent Falangist might do, adds, just in case, that Fermín is a good lad, someone to be trusted. Mir comes on strong and forces Carol to take the job. "It'll be good for you," he says, "you won't be drinking there, look what's happening to you, how sozzled you're getting, so off you go. If you give him what he wants, you'll have found a new client and you can eat some churros and enjoy yourself for a bit. It's not as if there's much happening on a rainy evening like this."

The scene in Panam's could end this way:

MIR (*to Carol*): Come on, you've got work to do. Didn't you hear? They're waiting for you at the Delicias cinema.

CAROL: I can't go. I don't have time . . .

MIR: You have to go, it's important. I'll tell you why later.

CAROL: But I have to pick up my boy.

MIR (*grabbing her chair*): What do you mean, your boy, for Christ's sake! I'll take you, come on!

CAROL: There's no need. I can go on my own.

MIR: Am I talking double Dutch? I said I'll take you.

CAROL: You go with your starry comrades, Ramón, and let me be.

MIR (*slaps her furiously*): Don't make a joke of this, or I'll break your neck. I've had it up to here with those fucking starry comrades and snowy mountains, but shit, I don't want anyone reminding me of it! (*Calming down*) The cinema is near my place, it's on my way. And don't look so miserable, damn it. You're going to eat some tasty churros, what more do you want?

Carol struggles to her feet. Encarnita gazes at her sadly.

9. DELICIAS CINEMA, 1947. EXTERIOR. DAY.

A luminous drizzle is falling. Outside the cinema, Carol opens a green umbrella and stares at the panel containing black-and-white stills from one of that week's films. She's wearing a black astrakhan coat, a very tight white skirt, a pink fake angora jersey, high-heeled shoes and black stockings.

Through the window of a taxi standing near the cinema, Ramón Mir watches her thoughtfully, cleaning his teeth with a toothpick. He signals to the taxi driver, and the cab pulls away.

The camera stays with Carol, who appears to have doubts about going inside the cinema. She turns on her heel and heads for the bar on the corner. Through the rain-streaked windows we see her order a glass of brandy at the bar, down it in one, apply lipstick while the other customers stare at her, then drink a second glass, pay, and go out into the street again.

She walks slowly back up the street and comes to a halt outside the cinema once more, studying the poster advertising the film: the silhouette of Gilda glows in the dark, as she smiles under a spotlight in her tight satin gown, a lit cigarette in her hand. Twirling the green umbrella above her head, Carol stares at the spirals of smoke curling upwards in the light, surrounding the beautiful golden mane of hair. She takes a small mirror and a lipstick out of her bag and retouches her lips. Unbuttoning her coat, she smooths down her jersey. A chubby, cheerful-looking man passes by. Without coming to a halt, he approaches her and whispers something we do not hear. She doesn't deign to look at him. Shortly afterwards, she goes into the cinema foyer closing her umbrella, asks the woman in the box office something, then starts to climb a dark, narrow side staircase (we begin to hear the whir of the projector and the soundtrack of the film: the song "Put the

Blame on Mame"). She pauses at the door to the projection booth. Before knocking, she raises her skirt, pulls up a black stocking, and adjusts the suspender on her thigh.

QUESTION to win five pesetas off Felisa: what's the name of the French actress who turned the act of removing her stockings and suspender belt on the edge of a bed into a fine art? Bet she doesn't know.

N.B.: Add references to Liberto Augé in the second version of this scene, which will need to be reworked as the director sees fit. For example, does Carolina Bruil know that her husband and Liberto Augé worked together in subversive activities for the committee of the clandestine C.N.T. union?

7

The first treatment of the script was starting to be structured around short, linked scenes, all of which seemed to me highly implausible in terms of narrative, but I was determined to look on the bright side. I have always believed that the truth, in fiction as in real life, occasionally arises out of something that doesn't make sense, is offered to us as a gift. I was under no illusion about the worth of the writing, and I found the result far from satisfactory – above all as a literary text, but who was going to care about that? – and all I can say in my defence was that I was strictly following what I had agreed with Héctor Roldán: there was no sign of any linear plot, and no incident or character drove the story on towards a climax, because there was no story to tell and no climax to resolve. In addition, the different elements making up this concoction didn't really blend together, and the narrative juxtaposed unconnected situations governed by what in the end did not claim to be anything more than a fiction camouflaged as a documentary (with a couple of concessions to the most pedestrian lyrical realism: Gilda's young fans and Carol's friend the blind prostitute), with the result that the supposed chronicle meandered on with a complete avoidance of suspense, and without any hint of narrative tension. No intrigue, no plot device leading to unlikely hypotheses as to the motive for the crime were present to disturb the lack of a link between characters who, as I have said, all blithely went their own ways. It was the proof of one of my favourite axioms: writing on commission for the cinema is like climbing a set of stairs: it can leave you flat on your back at any moment, because it is other people who decide whether or not they lead anywhere.

I persisted with my strategy of tiptoeing round the harsh nub of the story – the committing of the crime – and allowed Sicart to amuse himself in the sentimental and barely credible vagaries of his relationship with the prostitute, to the point where I began to wonder how much of his melancholy, painful evocation was pure fantasy. As I listened to him recall those fateful days I discovered that, in a somnambulist memory such as his, reconstructed under such suspicious and dire circumstances, the inconsistencies, lapses and tricks could be just as interesting as the truth. This was possibly because I was hearing his testimony about the tragedy at precisely the moment when the whole of Spain, in that summer of 1982, seemed determined to convert the bruised collective memory into a dangerous minefield. Sometimes, when he became tongue-tied or suddenly went blank, Sicart would remind me that he was still suffering from amnesia, and asked me to forgive him. It seemed to me that his calamitous clinical history disproved Friedrich Richter's famous dictum that memory is the only paradise we cannot be expelled from. He had been expelled once and for all.

"So it's a real problem," he said, and stared into space for a few seconds. "Well, I guess you know that I . . . I know how I did it, but don't ask me why. An odd case, isn't it?"

"Yes, I'm aware of that. And do you know something?" I said, to reassure him. "It's strange because there are many more cases in which the opposite happens. Lots of men know why they kill, but would be at a loss to explain how they've done it. Distinguished statesmen, for example, who believe they have persuasive reasons for killing, but claim that the way it's done has nothing to do with them."

"Fine. And do you think they really believe that?"

"I'm sure of it."

"Well, that had never occurred to me."

One morning, after my shower, I was pouring myself a cup of coffee in the kitchen when Felisa came in and announced there had been a call from Madrid while I was in the bathroom: Vilma Films Inc. They would call back. Shortly afterwards I was working at my desk in the study when the telephone rang again. I picked up and said in my best Marxian tone:

"And two hard-boiled eggs!"

This was followed by a silence at the other end of the line, and then:

"What was that? Who am I talking to?"

"Rufus T. Firefly here, the best-paid scriptwriter in the whole of Freedonia!"

"Ha ha, really funny," said M. V. Vilches, executive producer at Vilma Films. It was his fourth call in two days. "Don't you think you ought to control those Marxian excesses of yours, dear award-winning author?"

"It was a joke. How are you, Vilches? Are you calling from the capital of the kingdom or from Cinecitta?"

A snort.

"There's no reason I should be in Rome."

"Didn't you tell me you were trying to set up a co-production with Italy?"

"Ah, if you only knew just how many things I'm trying to set up . . ." He snorted once more, then his nasal voice took on the casual, falsely jocular tone so often heard in financial offices. "Well, let's not let that get us down. First and foremost, how is the work progressing?"

"Oh, very well. I've already got a title: 'Post-War Trains on a Track to Nowhere'. Don't you think that's great? It's one I've always liked. The only problem is, there are no trains in this movie."

"You're a real joker."

"Anyway," I hastened to add, "whatever it's called, it's going to be a memorable film, no doubt about it."

"Is it? Well, I've just been talking to Héctor and he's not so sure. He says that those thirty pages you sent him won't exactly set the world on fire."

"Is that what the director says? Well, they're only suggestions."

"Ah, but it seems they don't hang together," said M. V. Vilches. "Stick to the facts: that's what he recommended, if you remember?"

"Yes, but the facts aren't enough. Besides, I'm beginning to like all the techniques of a screenplay, the fades and segues, exteriors by day or by night, dialogues in-off, flashbacks. They're all novel, interesting narrative forms."

"It seems to me you've haven't understood what you're being asked to do. I advise you to talk to Roldán."

"Of course, whenever he likes."

"Didn't he tell you not to bother trying to plan the scenes? Listen, I've been in this business for years, and I know what I'm saying. Stop looking through the camera lens, Mr Griffith," he said mockingly.

"No, there's no way my eye is a camera. The thing is that yours truly here, just like Aristotle, finds it hard to think without images. But I'm well aware what a thingamajig . . . the first treatment of a screenplay is. It's a draft, a kind of synopsis."

"Obviously a first treatment can have dialogue and details, but I don't think they hired you to develop scenes that haven't yet been decided on . . . Anyway, it's none of my business." M. V. Vilches cleared his throat as if he were chuckling. "But tell me, why did you bring in those boys who are watching 'Gilda' in the cinema? What's the idea behind that?"

"I'm not sure yet. But they did exist; that's for real. Roldán wants realism, and those kids in the front row of the Delicias cinema, with the silvery light from the projector shining on their shaven heads, infected with dreams—"

"O.K.," he cut in. "And what about that blind prostitute who's a friend of the protagonist?"

"Oh, Encarnita. Sicart says she wasn't altogether blind. She could see a little, she had problems with an optic nerve or something . . . I hope the director likes her, she's another real person, and she can tell us about her friend Carolina and everything we can't see, important things that she remembers . . ."

"But don't you say she's blind? How are we going to believe someone who has no visual memory? What's she going to tell us, if she hasn't seen it . . .?"

"But she has. She creates her own images. Like in the cinema."

"I'm not sure, it doesn't sound very true to life. And those surreal dialogues of yours in a pick-up bar, with a drunken, disgraceful Falangist . . ."

"They're simply ideas. I did some research, found out a

few things. Apparently it all began in that place on the Rambla, which still exists. And that braggart Mir is real as well, just like the kids watching the film. That short scene in the cinema could be worth keeping, we'll see. At any rate, it takes place on the same evening as the crime, in the Delicias cinema and at the same time."

"So what?"

"So it's a touch of realism. Those boys are watching the film in the same cinema and on the same day as the crime takes place! And that film was 'Gilda'! It's a real fact, it's recorded in the trial proceedings and you can check in the film archives!" I exclaimed with my most enthusiastic, fake conviction. "Do you follow? We're bringing in real reality! And isn't that what the director wants?"

The producer did not share either my enthusiasm or my sense of humour.

"Fine, let's leave it . . ."

"Don't think I'm so keen on reality, I'm not. I don't understand why that particular muse is held in such high esteem. The sinking of the *Titanic* isn't any more memorable than that of the *Pequod,* don't you agree? My motto is that reality only exists if we're able to dream it."

"Listen, you can discuss all that with Héctor," Vilches snapped. "I called you about something else. I've just read your interview in the cultural supplement of *La Vanguardia.* Very original. Yes sir, really original."

"Oh, thanks. I thought you'd like it. It's very cinematographic."

"Really? Why's that?"

"Because the questions can't be seen, they're off screen. You know, that trick all good directors use. Suggest rather than show. And thanks . . ."

"Well, it looks as if you're having fun with your work," he said in a joking way, without bitterness.

"Yes. A little light relief."

"That's right. I'd no idea you were such a priest-hater."

"Well, I'm not much more than an amateur."

"Right. Let's hope it doesn't go any further."

"Are you worried that my healthy distaste will spoil the script?"

"Not at all. I'm not worried about your clowning around. You can mock the clergy or Spanish cinema as much as you like, I couldn't give a damn. Besides, as far as some of the poseurs I know are concerned, you'd be surprised how much I share your sarcastic attitude . . . The trouble is, those clever comments of yours could be very inopportune."

"Seriously?"

"You don't know this business. The film's financing hasn't been settled – the grant from the ministry is still up in the air, not to mention my arm-wrestling with the Vilma Films Inc. shareholders. Of course these are my problems not yours, but I'm perfectly within my rights to ask you to be more discreet when you talk about our project."

"Oh yes, of course. I was joking. But I don't understand how . . ."

"Indeed you do," Vilches said, his voice now sweet and cloying, as if he were sucking on a sweet. "It's very simple. In those official departments that hand out grants and permits – without which there won't be a film, and, by the way, if that happens you won't receive a penny more, in case you haven't realised that – in those offices there are people who don't see the funny side to your sarcasm and derision at all . . ."

"That I can understand."

"Now we're getting somewhere. But tell me: I'm curious to know where your attitude comes from? Does Spanish cinema really deserve all your mockery and spite?"

This dressing-down was starting to sound more like personal irritation, and that was beginning to get my goat. Of course I wasn't going to waste a minute explaining the shortcomings of Spanish cinema over the past forty something years. If M. V. Vilches, the most switched-on and international of our producers, still couldn't see that clearly, too bad for him and his films. So I decided to tease him a little more.

"Look, I can't help myself," I said pitifully. "It's stronger than me. And it's not a recent thing, believe me. When I was ten and used to go to the local cinema with my gang, I would split my sides laughing at all that clichéd Spanish *olé* stuff. And don't imagine it was because of any precocious critical insight, far from it! The thing is, our national films were pure comedy, even if it was unintended. Those historical movies by Juan de Orduña, for example. All those wigs and loopy patriotism made me laugh more than anything by Charlie Chaplin or the Marx brothers."

Silence at the other end of the line.

"That's not a good enough reason," Vilches said eventually. "Those embarrassing films of the past you mention have absolutely nothing to do with the cinema we're trying to make nowadays. Really, I don't understand your great need to do everything down."

"Alright, I'll tell you. But you won't believe me."

"Go on. Try me."

A residual compassion mixed with a great deal of verbal weariness prevented me going any further and earwigging the successful producer with the long list of "clichéd Spanish *olé* stuff" that I had been subjected to in my childhood, that purulent, sanctimonious nationalist Catholic cinema of the Forties and Fifties. So I said:

"It's the sound."

"The sound?"

"Yes, you heard. The sound in our Spanish films is so technically incompetent it hurts. And the actors' diction doesn't help. They don't project, and it's impossible to follow the dialogue. Or is it the sound engineers who are so bad? Between the two of them, they make me ill. Isn't it the same for you?"

A prolonged silence at the other end of the line.

"Are you still there, Mister Producer?"

I also asked, although this time it was a question I was asking myself: What are you doing, you dolt? Do you really want to throw away a more than generous fee for writing a few lines of rubbish . . . ? Until, like a sticky caterpillar crawling into my ear, came the distant voice of the executive producer of Vilma Films Inc. in his Madrid office gently taking a member of his staff to task over an order that had apparently not been carried out, and then excusing himself to me for the interruption and, in the same condescending tone he had used for his male or female colleague, reminding me that I was part of the team at Héctor Roldán's express wish, and that he only shared the director's high opinion of me up to a certain point. He added that, be that as it may, he would do all he could to defend the project and would argue with all those advisers who were not in the least inclined to share my sense of humour, and so it would be wise for me in the future to avoid such original, amusing declarations to the press.

"Do I make myself clear, esteemed writer?" he said.

"As clear as God in heaven."

"Good."

And with that, he hung up.

8

“Were there electroshocks?”

“By some miracle, I wasn’t prescribed them,” Sicart said. “Don’t forget that Ciempozuelos was an asylum full of chronic patients.”

“But you weren’t mad, and they must have known that.”

“They diagnosed a fit, a sudden mad impulse.”

“The fact is, your medical report doesn’t tell us a great deal.”

Sicart shrugged and sighed.

“Well, that’s all there is.”

All that evening he had been taciturn, reluctant to speak.

“Shall we talk today about what happened in the booth and—?”

“I don’t know, I don’t know,” he said. “First I’d like to get a few things clear.”

He’s going to tell me the story in dribs and drabs, I thought:

obviously, the more sessions we have, the more money he gets. But it could also be he finds it hard to summon such a crucial, painful memory. I tried another tack.

"Do you recall if during the trial they spoke of an 'unconscious impulse'?"

"No."

"Or 'dissociative reaction'?"

"No, not that either."

"Well, those were the terms used by Dr Tejero-Cámara and the other doctors . . ."

"Yes, I remember how they kept going on in that damnable jargon of theirs. But I never heard them say that. What is 'dissociative reaction'?"

"Something like finding ourselves impelled to do something without being able to distinguish between good and evil. It's an illness described as . . ." I glanced down at my notes, "an impulse that dilutes facts and establishes odd relationships with the cause."

He nodded, then shook his head, deep in thought.

"That bastard! That colonel medic gave me such a hard time, insisting I was suffering from hallucinations! He wanted me to tell him them, and never stopped asking questions, the son of a bitch! In the end I got so tired of it I told him that yes, I saw naked women on the walls. But what the fellow liked most of all was to talk about . . . What did he call it . . .? Ah, yes! The 'trigger factor'."

"Why such a . . . precise diagnosis?"

"I haven't the faintest idea."

He had asked Felisa for an iced coffee in a glass and was now drinking it. On the table was a bowl with ice cubes. He took two more and stirred the coffee with a finger. Frowning, he remained lost in thought, a faraway look in his eye. I added water to my whisky, adjusted the parasol to correct the shade, and looked through my notes, all to give him time to sift through his recollections.

"According to an initial medical report, your case is described as . . ." I read slowly from my notebook, "a homicidal impulse that represses all physical resistance and frees the hands without passing through the brain, which does not get involved in the act, and is not aware of what it is doing."

"I'm not sure," Sicart said, puzzled. "What I remember is that things went from bad to worse . . . When I was in Ciempozuelos, with the brutal treatment I received, I suffered from cerebral palsy, a sort of stroke, and all of a sudden I couldn't remember a stack of things that had happened to me. Things I had to learn about all over again."

"Such as?"

"Well, everything they told me that had happened, all the bad things they told me I did."

"Just a moment. Is what you're going to tell me what you actually remember you did, or what the doctors said you had done?"

"It's the same thing, isn't it?"

I could imagine his narrowed eyes behind the sunglasses.

"Are you sure?"

I certainly wasn't. I had enough information on the subject to know that the chief object of Dr Tejero-Cámara's most radical therapies, which in those days were promoted and financed by the Franco regime's repressive apparatus, was subtly to change, by means of a laborious mental process of dismantling and expiatory reconstruction, the meaning and intention of certain misdemeanours, especially if they were of Marxist-Leninist inspiration.

"Well, not everything they said to me," Sicart said with a faint, sly smile. "I added things of my own. I don't know if it figures in my medical report, but those endless interrogations got me so riled I pretended to be a degenerate just to get things over with."

"What do you mean exactly?"

"Well, playing the degenerate was very useful to me. To start with, it took my mind off the ordeal of the judicial mess, which I was very bitter about. And at the same time, it confused Dr Tejero-Cámara. He used to go on and on about the fateful neuronal bases of Marxism, of the predictable disorders caused by the libertarian way of life, and so on and so forth."

"According to that doctor's diagnosis, you were suffering from a pathology defined as 'Marxist cretinism'. It sounds like a joke."

"No, it isn't!" Sicart cut me short. "The colonel wasn't one for jokes. He was a savage brute, insisting on driving the demons from my brain! Anarcho-syndicalist demons, libertarian implants, or Marxist, or Catalan ones. That fellow saw post-war Barcelona as a hotbed of anarchism, whoring and lawlessness! I had to confess to some misdeeds to keep him happy and off my back."

"Misdeeds? Can you explain that?"

Felisa had just come out onto the terrace with a carpet and a beater. Sicart stared at her, as though suspicious of what she might be doing. One of the clothes lines was very slack, couldn't bear the weight of the carpet and came down. Felisa tightened it, and began beating the carpet energetically, while Sicart went on:

"The colonel thought that all the Red prisoners were mentally defective. I won't say that some weren't, but all of them? My goodness: with his theories about the degenerate nature of libertarian and Marxist neurones, the bastard was a ball-breaker. He wanted to cure us, to wipe away that defect. The first day, a nurse, obeying orders, gave me a tremendous beating. And with the chaplain's blessing, by the way. And the colonel never left me in peace, but spent the whole damned day interrogating the degenerate Red, as he called me, who had burned churches and read Bakunin and distributed the subversive *Tierra y Libertad* newspaper. Until you couldn't take it anymore and confessed just because you were exhausted.

As I was a work colleague of Señor Augé's, who was already locked in the clink, they insisted that at the age of seventeen I had been a member of a unit he commanded during the war that committed all kinds of outrages – something Augé always denied. And they also wanted to implicate me in a C.N.T. plot to shoot a police informant by the name of Eliseo Melis, who Señor Augé had mentioned to me at some point. Listen, that great eminence invented a whole crazy scenario intended, according to him, to wipe out our greatest sin, to bury it by confessing to our faults and anarcho-syndicalist machinations. Do you know what he advised me from the start? That I should never ask myself questions that might upset me. Avoid questions about that murder, don't think about that prostitute, don't take responsibility for that, he commanded me. No respect for justice, no political, moral or personal obligation can force you to do that, he would say, and anyway it won't alter your fate, because you're sure to be found guilty, nothing can save you from being garrotted. By not asking questions, you alleviate your degenerate spirit. He used to say that kind of thing. The fact is I must have seemed to him very degenerate, nothing more than a good-for-nothing whoremonger, because the interrogations were endless. But I knew how to deal with him, what he was after, so one day, when I couldn't stand it anymore, do you know what I did? I started inventing monstrous stories about Reds, Bolsheviks and so on . . . a load of nonsense . . ."

"But why did you do that?"

"No particular reason, just to get it over with. Those interrogations were so deadly, absolute torture. You had to try to cut them short. If you confessed spontaneously to some barbarity that a swine of an anarchist might commit – forcing a priest to drink a bottle of castor oil, for example, or violating a nun – they left you in peace for a few days."

"Seriously?"

"They asked you to write it all down, as therapy, if you follow me? It meant you could concentrate peacefully on that for a while, and they treated you more considerately. I was so fed up that I confessed to having raped two nuns during the Civil War. I made up the details about how and when it happened. It was all lies. Oh yes, I invented the whole lot; I remember I called one of them Sister Lucía, and the other Sister Angustias. They were nuns from the charterhouse at Montalegre de Tiana, and I said they were from Andalusia. One of them had a squint, and the other a bit of a limp . . . It was very simple. The medical team was very interested in anarcho-syndicalist outrages, and they saw the details as very important. I told them that Sister Lucía had spent the war hidden in an apartment in the Gràcia neighbourhood, protected by a devout couple who ran some sort of restaurant. Lucía helped in the kitchen, and it turned out that she liked cooking so much that when the Nationalists came she didn't want to return to the convent, and besides she was pregnant by a butcher who used to sweet-talk her, and the two of them eventually opened their own place. Dr Tejero-Cámara found the story really fascinating."

"I can imagine," I said. "But let's see—"

"I also pretended I was queer for a while."

"You don't say."

"Yes, because in the canteen I saw that the queers were given two helpings of chicken wings! Shit, they had it easy! And it was so simple! I concocted a jumble of vices and atrocities typical of Reds, and it worked a treat. I don't like to say so, but I came to enjoy pulling the wool over the psychiatrists' eyes with all that rubbish."

"But that must have been added to your file, to make the sentence worse. Didn't you care?"

"No. Because I was sure they were going to sentence me to death anyway. They were going to garrotte me."

There was no point my questioning the veracity of his story, because I had already settled myself more or less comfortably on another level of respect for the truth: that of credibility, which is something that writing obliges me to respect, and which in the end is more important to me than any reality. Sicart's story was no doubt like a sleepwalker's, manipulated and reconstituted, and it was quite likely that all the others I still had to hear would be the same. I understood that, in a testimony as well-worn as that of an ex-prisoner, the links between words and truth could now only be established by means of a credible manipulation, in other words thanks to a further recreation and restoration, because the story came to me from an undeniable personal tragedy, but was also rooted in the fraught memory of the dark days of the dictatorship, the resentment, humiliation, pain and desire for revenge that still persisted in many different guises in the collective subconscious.

In other words, perhaps things didn't happen exactly that way, but this was how Fermín Sicart, a reconstructed mystery, a man who did not really know how to assume his past, recollected them.

"You know, nowadays I'm a bit ashamed of the rubbish I made up," Sicart said. Glancing at my notebook, he added with a hint of expectation: "Are you going to write all that down, as I've said it?"

"I don't know, but don't worry: what is seen or heard in the film won't have any legal repercussions. Besides, I don't think your stay in Ciempozuelos will even be included in the movie; that's not what it's about."

"Ah, I understand."

"Well, it's late. Shall we leave it for today?"

"Whatever you like." Without hurrying, he took off his sunglasses, rubbed his eyes and got wearily to his feet. "Let's see if tomorrow I can remember things that might interest you more."

"I'm sure you will."

*

The following day he had a sore throat, and Felisa made him some lemon juice with honey. For the next couple of sessions he kept clearing his throat, and quite often stopped talking altogether. Curiously, this only added to the strange power of conviction of what he was saying, despite the occasional inventions and inconsistencies.

I still had my doubts about Sicart's reliability as a chronicler, and I soon realised that my work was heading in a direction that was perhaps not without interest, but wasn't what I had agreed with Héctor Roldán when we established the basis of the screenplay. I wondered whether Sicart was really going to be a great help, and to what extent it was convenient to base the scarce facts about the murder on his testimony, because as soon as the possibility arose of discovering a motive for the crime (even though that was not the objective of my work), his persistent lack of memory – whether this was congenital or had been induced by the shock therapy was still to be resolved – meant that it all fell apart.

I imagined his mind to be like an antiquated dressing table with the memory drawers mixed up; where you expected to find shirts there were socks, and where there should have been socks, underpants. I began to think there might be a better way to get at the complete truth: supposing Sicart's mental lapses or involuntary distortions were really not genetic in origin but induced – that is, they were the shadowy remains of a memory that had been expurgated, usurped and then reconstituted as a result of the severe shock treatment he had received in the Ciempozuelos asylum, the consequences of which had already been evident during his trial – wouldn't it be worthwhile to start considering that forced loss of memory that was both manipulated and recreated, or grafted on, so to speak, as the essential basis of the story, its most interesting and truthful aspect?

"The accused declares he has no memory of what led him to kill the prostitute," according to one of the newspapers from the time that I consulted. "I remember how and where I did it, but I've forgotten why," read another headline.

That was what Sicart declared then and was still maintaining now. Words that sounded sincere, but which still left me feeling there was something fishy going on. How could someone remember the details of something so terrible – a murder by strangling, no less – and not remember why they had done it? Could there really be a therapy able to bury in oblivion the reason that led him to commit the murder, the motive or lack of it that led him to such horror, while at the same time preserving such a detailed memory of how he did it?

In addition, I couldn't get the confusion over the cigarette case out of my mind. It was only a moment, but during that brief instant Sicart had really believed it was mine. How did that mix-up arise? Could it be the start of senile dementia that he was trying to hide from me so as not to miss out on the money I was paying, or was it due to whatever they might have inoculated him with thirty years earlier in Ciempozuelos? Besides, I was well aware that to remember is to interpret, to see the things of the past in a certain way. So I needed to keep my wits about me.

However that might be, it occurred to me that perhaps Roldán was not so wide of the mark with his idea about the toxic soap bubbles that needed to be burst, because on occasion my interlocutor seemed mentally to find himself inside a bubble that was as iridescent and shiny as it was erratic and fickle.

9

The following Monday morning I worked half-heartedly on a key scene set in the projection booth of the Delicias cinema, lay down for a while on the sofa, read an article on the political transition that predicted rifts and disasters all over the place, then went for a swim.

The water's embrace was not as warm as on other occasions; the weight of my doubts and suspicions affected my speed and rhythm. At that time of day there was usually no-one in the pool apart from Señora Falp, a little old grandmother with blonde hair and a cat-like expression. She was a lively woman with scrawny arms and legs, but in the water she was unbeatable; she could swim three lengths in the time it took me to do one, and alternated crawl with elegant breast- and backstroke. It was nothing new for me to see myself humiliated by this fearsome old woman, always fit and competitive in her pink bathing cap and suit, especially when she displayed her backstroke, her body rocking slightly from side to side, slithering through the water like an eel, an irrepressible smile on her face. In her right ear shone an earring stud with a single ruby in it, which glinted even beneath the endless whirl of foam and bubbles that always accompanied this ancient mermaid. As we crossed halfway down the pool, she was swimming crawl and her tiny fish's mouth appeared on the surface of the water beneath her sagging armpit. She smiled at me and said:

"I've done fifty lengths! What about you?"

"What was that?" I stammered. "I can't hear."

"Try the sauna. That's the best thing when you're feeling weak!"

I agreed, but by then she was ten metres away and didn't hear me.

I finished sooner than usual and was home by half past one. I ate without much appetite and won a bet with Felisa, who had greeted me with a sarcastic riddle:

"'There's no place like home . . .'"

"Judy Garland in 'The Wizard of Oz'."

"Damn it!" She didn't like to lose. "I owe you five pesetas."

Before I shut myself in my study again, Felisa informed me she had picked up another two cigarette butts on the terrace, in a pot with carnations next to where Sicart and I had been sitting. She informed me that there was no way she was going to collect any more butts from any damn pot.

"It wasn't me!" I said. "I promise."

The amnesiac murderer arrived punctually at five. I spent some time watching him through the study window, for some unknown reason postponing the moment when I confronted him. I saw him pacing stealthily around the terrace, lost in thought. Eventually he went to sit under the parasol, hands behind his back and head lowered, staring at the seat where I usually sat. Felisa approached him cloth in hand, and, as she began to wipe the marble tabletop, asked if he would like a coffee.

"No thanks," Sicart said. "But I'd really welcome a beer, Señora Eloísa. If it's no bother."

"No bother at all. But my name is Felisa."

"Of course, I'm sorry." He gave a little laugh. "I don't know what's going on recently, I keep forgetting names. It must be the aftermath of that therapy that scrambled my brains."

"You have memory lapses, Señor Picart. A symptom of senile dementia. At our age, it's to be expected."

"No, not a bit of it. Forgetting a name doesn't mean you're demented. Not at all!"

"That's how it starts, Señor Ricart, you can be sure of it."

"Good God, no! Yours truly has seen no sign of that!"

"Pleased to hear it," Felisa said, wiping the table vigorously. She lifted the ashtray to clean underneath it, then dropped it back on the table with a dull thud. "But once your memory starts to go . . ."

"But that's not the case, Señora! It's . . . something else."

"That's how it might seem, Señor Guitart—"

"Sicart."

"—but it's a sure sign of illness, I'm telling you." Felisa shook the cloth, even though there was nothing to shake out of it. She smiled slyly and said: "Would you like the beer in an iced glass? Shall I bring you a bigger ashtray? Answer my second question first."

"No. I mean, it's not necessary, I can manage with this one." He fell silent, bewildered. "Señora, I have to admit, I don't always understand your little jokes."

Felisa shook her head resignedly and beat a retreat.

"Sit back," she ordered him. "I'll bring you your beer straightaway."

"Fine. Thank you." Leaning back in his seat, he linked his hands behind his head and watched Felisa out of the corner of his eye. When he was sure she was out of earshot, he muttered to himself: "Yes, thank you very much, Señora E-looo-iii-sa."

The weather that afternoon was very hot but unsettled, with a dull, ragged light as if rain and sun were entwined in the air. I strode out onto the terrace, extended my hand to him and sat down with my notebook and a biro. For the first time I also set up a tape recorder, which Sicart regarded warily. I wanted a detailed description of how the crime had been committed, including the sordid parts, but I'd decided to approach the matter delicately so as not to make him feel uncomfortable, starting with a topic that was of little interest to me, or so I thought. While I was consulting my notes, Felisa arrived with the beer for him and a whisky and water for me. She remained standing behind Sicart, clutching the tray to her chest. I switched on the tape recorder.

"Let's see. Before Carolina Bruil appeared in your life, Señor Sicart, in the year . . ." I noticed how pale my whisky was. When I took a sip, it was almost all water, so I glanced sternly at Felisa before I went on. "In 1945, you were interrogated at police headquarters concerning certain activities of your work colleague Liberto Augé, who at that time was being investigated by the Politico-Social Brigade."

"Yes, that was a real bore."

"I was struck by something you said then." I signalled discreetly to Felisa, who began reluctantly to withdraw. "Something very shocking . . ."

"Ah, I'm not surprised. That interrogation was dreadful. I realised from the outset that they wanted to stitch up the old man, so I started mixing everything together and making things up just to confuse them. And boy, did I confuse them!" He waited for Felisa to go inside and added: "I told them, 'You're wrong: Señor Augé isn't an anarchist, and he never has been. He's just a queer! Haven't you seen the way he walks? He's a poof!' They were stunned, they hadn't reckoned on my little bombshell. 'Is he really a queer?' they kept asking. They started wondering about it, and couldn't decide. They didn't get anything out of me."

"But Señor Augé wasn't a homosexual."

"Of course not! He was a real man, with balls. But I fooled all those idiots."

"I see. Anyway, just now I wasn't talking about what you said about Liberto Augé, but about someone else."

I insisted I had been struck that even then, when he had not yet heard of Carol, he had declared that he knew the man she was married to, a fugitive from justice by the name of Jesús Yoldi.

"Oh that. It was pure chance," Sicart said. "He came to the cinema to see Señor Augé, not me. They were friends. I didn't know him at all. How could I imagine that years later I would fall for his widow? All the police told me at the time was that he used a pseudonym and that he was dangerous, an anarchist capable of anything."

"How did you come to meet him?"

"Pure chance, as I said. He came to the cinema one evening, knocked on the projection booth door and asked for the operator Augé. He said he was a friend of his, and needed to talk to him urgently. I remember it was raining heavily and he was soaked . . . I never saw him again after that day."

According to the case file, the facts were as follows: one rainy day in May 1945, in the middle of the evening session, a man who said his name was Jesús Yoldi appeared at the projection booth at the Delicias cinema asking for his friend Liberto Augé. His young colleague, Fermín Sicart, told him that Señor Augé was not there and that he did not know if he would be coming in, because in recent days he had not been feeling well. He also declared that he had never seen the visitor before, and that his visit could not have come at a worse moment, because he arrived just as the first reel of a poorly synchronised Cantinflas movie was coming to an end, and there had been an electricity blackout, and everything pointed to it being a stormy session. Sicart affirmed that this stranger not only looked pitiful, he also looked very odd: he had a threadbare wig on his head, and was wearing rice-powder make-up, like some ageing, half-crazy silent screen star, his hair silver at the temples and with what looked like a fake goatee beard and moustache, painted lips and eye-brows that had run in the rain. His half-open raincoat revealed a peasant's costume, with a black sash and waistcoat, corduroy trousers and espadrilles.

"He looked like a drenched scarecrow," Sicart told me, "and his face looked as if he had just been beaten up. In fact, as Señor Augé later explained, the fellow was in disguise, because the bloodhounds from the Politico-Social Brigade were on his trail. He was, or had wanted to be, an actor, and on Sundays he performed in one of those amateur theatres, you know, a former workers' co-operative in Gràcia called El Cor de l'Aliança, I think. He used to go there already made-up and in costume so that he wouldn't be recognised in the street. But also – although I didn't know it at the time – that day he was suffering from an attack of jealousy. I remember his eyes were glittering like gimlets, one bigger than the other."

A few days later, Señor Augé told him the stranger was a union colleague with whom he shared information and propaganda tasks, that he had been reported to the police by a Fascist neighbour, which was why he went round in disguise and had been sleeping for a while at a friend's place as a precaution. According to Señor Augé, he was a determined, courageous man who was a prominent member of the C.N.T., and yet, Sicart insisted, on the day of his visit he looked a terrible mess.

"He asked if he could wait for Señor Augé there in the booth, and he looked so rough I couldn't say no. He sat down and seemed to be enjoying himself with the bird and listening to Cantinflas' patter. He kept screwing up his nose and rubbing his eyes; I thought it was because of the smell of the acetone, but it wasn't. A short while later he buried his face in his hands and I saw he was weeping . . . I didn't know what to do. I took the bottle out of the cupboard and offered him a glass of wine, but he didn't want one. The noise from the projector was getting to him, so I told him he would be better off waiting for Señor Augé downstairs in the cinema. He didn't respond. Half an hour later he grew tired of crying and left without a word."

By the time Señor Augé returned to work five days later, Sicart had learned what had happened. He had been interrogated at the Travessera de Dalt police station concerning his relationship with Braulio Laso Badía, alias Jesús Yoldi, and above all, about his death, which had occurred two days earlier. Because on Tuesday 14, three days after his visit to the Delicias cinema, the man calling himself Jesús Yoldi had hanged himself in a pergola on Calle Legalidad, on the flat roof of a building whose inhabitants said they did not know him and had never seen him before. According to the police, the reason for this fateful decision was that he discovered his wife was cheating on him with another man. Apparently, the evening when he turned up at the Delicias cinema, perhaps hoping Señor Augé could offer him some comfort, he had been following her in the rain from the moment she left home, and had seen her with her lover in a bar on Calle Mayor in Gràcia. The two of them were behaving in a way that left no room for doubt, especially the man, a member of the Falange in his black uniform, boots and belt, and probably a pistol as well.

"Well, that's not how the police would have put it to Señor Augé, of course," Sicart said. "Those bastards are all the same, they back each other up, but I see things differently. At any rate, Señor Augé told them he knew nothing about any of it and didn't know the woman who had betrayed his friend, he hadn't even known he was married or was living as a couple. In fact, it came as a complete surprise to him. I can still see him shedding tears of pity for his colleague and at the same time cursing him. He was annoyed his friend had hidden the fact that he lived with a variety artiste, a dancer or trapeze artist or something of the sort, a young woman with a child. He must have wanted to protect her just in case he was arrested someday, but old Augé couldn't understand why he had never told him. Maybe he was ashamed of her?"

He broke off when he heard the telephone ring in my study. It rang four times before Felisa answered it. Sicart adjusted his glasses on his nose and drank the beer straight from the bottle. He coughed, nodded sadly, and went on:

"So in a fit of jealousy he hanged himself. According to the police, he left a letter explaining everything, putting the blame on the woman he loved. But do you know the saddest part?" Sicart paused, still nodding. "The poor devil killed himself for nothing. I mean, there was no reason for him to be jealous. It was all a stupid misunderstanding."

Felisa was hurrying out towards us.

"A misunderstanding?" I asked.

"That's right. I only learned about it much later on, but it shook me as if it had happened right that minute . . . the worst thing that could happen to a man in love!"

He removed his glasses and rubbed his eyes before glancing up at Felisa, who had just come to a halt in front of him, although her message was for me.

"Urgent call from Madrid."

"The producer Vilches?"

"His secretary."

This was the second call in less than an hour. I sensed that it was bad news, but I was caught up with Sicart and his distracted nodding, his struggle with his memories, about to reveal something important. Or so I thought.

"Tell her I'm not back yet."

"She won't believe me."

"Then tell her I'm in the shower. That I'll call back later."

Sicart was still nodding, lost in thought. Felisa stood there for a few seconds, staring at him with barely concealed suspicion, as though she didn't believe a word he said. Then she turned on her heel and left.

"As I was saying," Sicart continued, "I heard about the misunderstanding two years later, thanks to Encarnita . . ." He closed his eyes, cleared his throat and all of a sudden his voice seemed to be coming from the bottom of a deep well. It sounded muffled and distant the more he tried to string together an explanation that surfaced only with great difficulty, with pauses for reflection in the midst of a lot of nonsense about alleged good intentions, mix-ups, the dirty tricks played by fate, or the remorse he shared with his victim; words half whispered and half spat out, beneath which it seemed to me there lurked a sense of guilt – not for his crime, not for having taken the life of the woman he loved, more for not having noticed the never-ending loneliness and sadness of her existence, for not having taken a closer interest in her misfortune or having helped her sufficiently. If only he had known that the poor wretch disguised as a peasant who had come to his projection booth that day was her husband! Or if Encarnita had known Carol and the tragic consequences of the misunderstanding two years earlier, when her friend began to work as a prostitute! Because then Sicart would have been able to take responsibility in time for the whole sad story. But when he first held her in his arms there was already little he could do. She had already taken to drink, her son had died, and she had lost her job and all hope with it. She was already resigned to her fate and to the deceitful protection offered by her executioner, Mir the Falangist, who ended up stripping her of all her willpower by means of who knew what lies, promises and probably even threats. By the time Sicart fully understood the story of the tragic misunderstanding she had caused, she was already on a downward slope and there was little to be done to restore her self-esteem, however much one loved her.

You could see the sadness of the whole world in her oriental eyes, Sicart said, even when she laughed. It was because he felt so sorry for her when he saw how sad she was that he commented on it to Encarnita. She explained to him why she drank so much and why she had handed herself over entirely to that animal of a lover after she had lost her one true love, whose death she blamed herself for. That poor wretch had committed suicide because he couldn't bear for her to betray him with a Falangist: that was the painful truth. But, as Encarnita revealed, that truth concealed an even more painful one.

"The thing is, Carol was only trying to help him," Sicart said.

The fact was, he added, she was only trying to help by becoming friendly with the councillor Ramón Mir Altamirano, the neighbourhood political boss, the mummy from the "Mummiment" as several wits in the local tavern called him, although out on the street they feared and respected him. She knew him by sight because Mir often went to the variety shows at the Salón Guinardó, where Carol performed several times that winter under the theatrical name of Chen-Li, the lovable Puss in Boots. Sicart could still remember her image on the posters displayed in neighbourhood bars and stores, as well as in the Delicias box office. Trying to surprise me with his unstable memory (which he had already proved was not that poor, depending on what was involved, by reeling off the complete Barcelona team of the day: Miró, Zabala, Benito, Raich, Rosalench, Franco, Sospedra, Escolá, Martín, César and Bravo) he jokingly recreated an attractive and entirely plausible programme for the theatre that perhaps would have interested our director Roldán, who was so addicted to his cursed real events. It was more or less the following:

SALÓN GUINARDÓ, 43, Escarnalbou.

February 5/6, 1945, Saturday evening, Sunday matinée and evening. Top-Class Variety Acts: CONCHITA LUCENA, classical Spanish dancer. MATARI, mimic and comedian. PROFESSOR FASSMAN, international magician and psychic. RUFIÁN and

TARDÁ, world-famous clowns and acrobats. CARMEN DE GRANADAS, the artiste personifying Andalusian art. CHEN-LI, PUSS IN BOOTS, exotic dancer and acrobat. PILAR RAJOLA, verbal contortionist and radio comedienne. PATRICIA GARBANCIO, renowned tango-sardana dancer. ANTONIO AMAYO, the bronze little gypsy, the public's favourite. Tickets: 1.50 pesetas.

"The same crazy artistes who performed in the Selecto and Moderno cinemas. I can still see their names on the billboards," Sicart said. "What a bunch! But we'd better get back to the important stuff. Let's rewind."

Wearily, he described the Falangist Ramón Mir Altamirano, stressing what a show-off and what a theatre lover he was. He was a sex-mad addict of variety shows, and never missed one of the Cat's performances. He wanted to get off with her, and had tried it on umpteen times, as she herself told Encarnita: she forced herself to let him sweet-talk her and even flirted with that pompous ass in the hope that she could get some support or recommendation for her man, who had been living in hiding and under a false name for some time because the police were looking for him.

"All she wanted to do was help the man she loved out of his mess," Sicart explained. "That was why she accepted Mir's invitations, to tell him her troubles and arouse his compassion, to explain to him tearfully that her husband had been unjustly reported by a neighbour, a vengeful former boyfriend . . . She thought the Falangist would help her."

"She was really naive, wasn't she? What could she expect from a creep like that?"

"Yes, but she thought it was worth a try . . ."

"Besides, it was no joke. There was a warrant out for her husband's arrest, wasn't there?"

"Yes, I believe there was."

"Then she really was naive."

Sicart shrugged resignedly.

"What else could she do, poor thing? She did what many people did in those days, beg for favours from whoever was in charge, be it a Falange bigwig or a little shit like Mir. It was common back then, lots of families suffered humiliations like that."

I had to understand Carol's good faith and how shameless the Falangist was, Sicart insisted. Mir claimed to be in a position of authority and to be well connected. He led her to believe that her husband's case wasn't serious, that he could use his influence in the upper echelons and possibly get the case reviewed, make a recommendation, or at least find some extenuating circumstance that would whitewash the defendant's union past – provided of course that he gave proper demonstration of his unswerving allegiance to the regime, testimony which Mir himself was willing to endorse. He even took her with him on several occasions to the provincial Falange headquarters on Paseo de Gràcia, boasting of how influential he was there, and telling her of his contacts in the Civil Government and the military prosecutor's office. He assured her that if on her husband's charge sheet there were no acts of violence – which appeared to be the case – then more than likely the affair would be archived. Carol did all this without telling her husband, because she knew he would never have agreed, and because from the start she could guess what Mir would ask her for in exchange, and she didn't want to think too much about it, or to feel intimidated: she was ready to make any sacrifice. She had three or four dates with him in the Monumental Bar on Calle Mayor in Gràcia, and eventually saw she would have to go the whole way, and so allowed herself to be taken to a cheap hotel behind Plaza Lesseps. And this turned out to be the rainy afternoon that Jesús Yoldi followed her in the street . . ."

"Yes, she must have been an extraordinary woman." I fell silent, then suggested: "But don't you think it was strange she was so willing to sacrifice herself? Unless of course . . . well, it's just occurred to me. Unless she had already had some experience in the world of prostitution."

I caught a glimpse of Sicart's wrinkled eyelids drooping sadly behind his dark glasses.

"There's no evidence of that," he said curtly. "Besides, that was impossible. She was never a whore like the others."

"I understand." For a few moments I said nothing, then returned to the attack: "So how did the police come to find out that the story of his jealousy was not what it seemed?"

"I don't know. But the police had been on his trail for a while. When I told Señor Augé everything I'd heard from Encarnita, he refused to believe it. Señor Augé always claimed Carol was with that Falangist Mir because she was a whore and a bitch, and that she didn't arrange to meet him in the Monumental Bar to save her husband from jail, but to denounce him . . . He was wrong, of course . . ."

"And didn't Augé ever accuse her of it when he saw her with you?"

"I think he only saw her once, and then he felt sorry for her because she was so drunk. And the last thing she wanted to do, of course, was to tell the truth about what was going on to Señor Augé or anybody else . . ."

"Well, there's a report that doesn't fit with that. In Augé's file it states that Carolina Bruil, in the years you knew her, used to frequent the police station on Travessera de Dalt together with Ramón Mir, probably at his instigation, because he had already turned her into an informant."

"I never believed anything of the kind," Sicart swiftly contradicted me. "Those bastards in the Politico-Social Brigade invented that because it suited them. They were never able to prove anything. But she was incapable of doing that, you can bet your life on it. She was a good woman. She didn't give away her husband, and there was no reason why she should denounce or compromise Señor Augé either."

"Are you sure?" I consulted my notes once more. "Do you remember when she lost an earring in your booth?"

Sicart raised a hand to his throat and shook his head.

"I'm not sure. Let's see . . . wasn't that the day she arrived with a tremendous hangover?"

I reminded him of the facts. According to the police, Liberto Augé, the old anarchist then suspected of being a member of the C.N.T.'s illegal Public Entertainments Union and under close surveillance, entered the Delicias cinema on the morning of August 3, 1947, where he loaded the film reels and checked the projector. He had been performing these maintenance tasks for some time, leaving everything ready for the evening session, which his colleague Fermín Sicart dealt with. In addition, the file on the activities of the prostitute Carolina Bruil Latorre revealed that, on the evening of that same day, she visited Sicart in his booth and allowed him to have his way with her in exchange for a frugal meal and a small amount of money. Prior to this, she had asked her client to allow her to go and fetch some beers from the bar on the corner, where her lover R.M.A. was waiting for her. He bought her several glasses of wine and gave her instructions: she was to go back and join Sicart and at what she considered an opportune moment was to say to him that she had lost an earring and pretend to look for it everywhere in the booth. That would give her the chance to search the sacks of films Augé had received that morning.

"All of which," I said, "points to the fact that, encouraged by Mir (although the police report does not specify the reasons for the search), she was likely to find copies of *Solidaridad Obrera*, the C.N.T.'s clandestine newspaper, hidden in the sacks, as well as envelopes with money. According to the file on him, one of the tasks assigned to Augé back then was to collect the subscriptions of union members, as well as distributing prisoners' correspondence to their families. So she—"

"No, no, no," muttered Sicart. "Carol would never have done that."

"Don't forget, she was a police informant."

"But don't you see? The whole thing was invented by those bastards in the Politico-Social Brigade!" After this explosion, Sicart calmed down, then said: "Anyway, if she ever did anything of the sort, she was forced into it by that lowlife pimp of hers. Wrong-headed or not, everything Carol did, first for her husband and then for her poor sick boy and for herself, was always with the best of intentions . . ."

"I understand. But tell me something: after all that had happened, does it seem logical to you that she would really get together with that disgusting individual, Mir?"

"I don't know what to say. I never dared even ask myself that."

"Do you think she could have done it as . . . some kind of atonement?"

Sicart shook his head, confused.

"What do you mean? Listen, those were dreadful times, and you had to get by as best you could. If you had to sell your soul to escape from poverty, then so be it. If Carol ended up getting together with that son of a bitch, she must have done so to escape from hardship, and for her son's sake. I'm sure of it. That's what I've always thought."

Although I had my doubts, I said nothing, because I could see he was also troubled by suspicions. In that woman's heart there can only have been a bitter residue of sex and remorse. As for the Falangist Mir, with her he must have been living a mixture of furtive lovemaking and lost starry ideals.

Behind my back I heard the snick of secateurs. When I turned, I saw Felisa stealthily pruning the pots of ferns at the far end of the terrace, muttering to herself.

"I've got it," we heard her murmur. "The youth of today . . ."

"She must be working out some riddle or other," I told Sicart.

We had continued our conversation longer than usual, and dusk was falling. I called an end to the interview, switched off the tape recorder and offered him another beer. He refused, saying he was in a bit of a hurry. He got to his feet annoyed with himself, grumbling in a low voice: "Let's see if tomorrow I can remember things better, dammit." Before leaving, though, he stood for a while smoking by the balustrade, his dark glasses pushed up on his forehead, watching as the first shadows descended on the city, perhaps sorting out his recollections in the black hole of a presumably forced and redirected amnesia, at the same time trying to espy the hazy outline of another city stretching way beyond what his eye could see, the condemned grey city of his condemned memory. A distant, phantom, wintry but indestructible city that was as obsolete but as persistent in his mind as it was in mine. And perhaps that was the reason why, seeing him standing there peering at the fading daylight as though expecting some signal from it, I suddenly felt that something I couldn't define was pushing me to put myself in his shoes and to look at the city with his disillusioned eyes and from his own fragile perspective: both of us perplexed and expectant with regard to the past and with our backs turned to the future. I imagined myself as having lived that horror, having been there that fateful day, having felt myself impelled to kill . . . Even though the sense of loss or being uprooted couldn't be the same, since destiny had been far more severe with him than with me, I did feel that the labyrinth of memory loss he was ensnared in could not and should not be completely alien to me.

Once he had gone, I was alone on the terrace. I tried to impose order on some images to see what kind of narrative structure might come out of them that I could add to the screenplay. I was bemused by an overabundance of facts and information that were probably of no use to me at all. What did I really have? A trite melodrama, a clumsy epic based on one woman's desperate spirit of sacrifice, a tale dripping with sentimentality and a few pornographic touches. In other words: a poor variety artiste who is not very bright agrees to go to bed with a fatuous, gutless Falangist who promises to intercede on her behalf in favour of her beleaguered husband. The husband, thinking he has been betrayed by this valiant woman, commits suicide. Two years later, she has lost everything and prostitutes herself, exploited by her presumed benefactor, until one day she dies, strangled by a new lover without any apparent motive.

I did not lose sight of the fact that this tragic story was not to turn into the film's plot in any way, even if the temptation to violate that prohibition was almost constant. For example: seeing that a fair amount of the information about the suicide came from police files and enquiries, was it utterly absurd to imagine a plot hatched by the Politico-Social Brigade in order to cast the whole responsibility onto Carolina Bruil? Could not the letter left by Jesús Yoldi explaining why he was going to hang himself have just as easily been written by somebody else? And there were multiple other subplots that could end up leading nowhere, other loose ends that doubtless would make Roldán happy, providing him with those toxic soap bubbles bequeathed to us by the Franco regime, and which the intrepid director was so keen to burst. Disposable material which in fact was not so ridiculous: a tender story of love and sacrifice wrapped up in the grey years of the

Forties, a sort of psychological and police *trompe l'oeil* inside a deceitful bubble, all ready to go . . . pop!

Be that as it may, the approach we had originally envisaged – opening up several theoretical approaches without exhausting any of them – seemed destined to get me nowhere, foretelling the worst possible outcome: creating expectations about the crime that would end up being frustrated, since the basic theme, so beloved of Héctor Roldán, was precisely this: that in this country nothing happens, nothing ever happens. Every now and then my conscience was troubled: you're setting the viewer up for something you're not going to give him, I told myself, when what you'd really like to do is set him or her up for something he wasn't expecting, even if you yourself do not know what that might be.

Should I persist in trying to find the truth behind the mask, when that truth was much less interesting than the mask itself? That was not what I was being paid for.

10

I suspended my swimming sessions for a fortnight because of the otitis I often suffer from. Felisa went on and on about it until I finally went to see a specialist. In the waiting room was an old couple I had coincided with a couple of times before. Neither of them tried to engage me in conversation, and between the two of them there was a solid, well-established silence. Sitting opposite each other, they were leafing absent-mindedly through old magazines: he was very relaxed, his legs stretched out; she was hunched over, concentrated on her reading. At a certain moment the woman stopped reading, stared at her husband's feet, and said:

"You've put those horrible yellow socks on again."

The man did not seem to hear her, and carried on reading. After a while, the woman said:

"Last week I bought you a pair of grey ones. Why don't you wear them?"

The man drew up his legs and looked down at his feet.

"These are the ones, Cloti. Look, I'm wearing them."

"They're yellow."

"No they're not. They're grey. Take a proper look."

Silence again. After a moment, she said:

"I bought them for you on Friday, I remember . . ."

"No, it was Wednesday. I know because it's the day I play pétanque with that good-for-nothing brother of yours."

Frowning, disbelieving, she went back to her magazine. Not for long.

"Look, Oriol, there's an interview here with that author of grey novels you like so much . . ."

"Black novels, you mean."

"No, I know perfectly well what I'm saying. Grey novels."

"Well then, I'm not interested," he said. Then, as if summoning up his patience, he added: "Haven't I told you a thousand times that the black or noir novel as they call it in French is the best way to investigate social conflicts, explore the human condition, to denounce implacably the injustices and corruption of our society?"

His wife interrupted him. "There you go again with your nonsense, Oriol!"

At this the man fell silent. Grumbling to himself, he buried his nose in what he was reading.

(For now, this dialogue doesn't fit into my treatment, because it seems quite unconnected to the main theme. But the way things are going . . . Who knows?)

When I arrived home, I poured myself a whisky in the study and rang Carmen. No news in Amsterdam. Bike rides along Utrechtsestraat, visits to the Van Gogh museum, pleasant outings, the kids fine, writing postcards all day, did you get Van Gogh's ear drawn by your youngest? Cousins very welcoming, weather splendid.

"How are you getting on with the film?" she said. "Have they fired you yet?"

"For the moment, they're respecting me."

"And how are things with Felisa?"

"Terrible. She's fleecing me every day."

"Tell her not to forget to water my petunias . . ." She broke off when she heard a sudden explosion of voices. "Will you be quiet a minute, kids?" A gentle telling-off, and then: "Haven't you had to go to Madrid?"

"No way! Listen, what's going on here in Catalonia is bad enough, but in Madrid it's a total farce. We're living in historic times!"

"Stop it, will you?" Carmen protested. "Even here they're talking about our transition, you know. Everyone asks me and I—"

"Tell them it's all going great guns. Only a little more than a year after those Civil Guard clowns burst into Congress, and they're selling Saint Teresa's miraculously preserved arm in a raffle."

"You're such an idiot! Go on, pass me to Felisa."

I said goodbye, called Felisa to the telephone, and went into the kitchen for more ice. When Felisa had finished, I called Madrid and the news M. V. Vilches had for me confirmed my fears. Negotiations were stuck, government grants and patronage were frozen, and the film's production plans would have to be modified. The previous week an agreement had finally been signed to bring fresh capital on board, so that now the film had an associate producer, someone by the name of Edgardo Mardanos. He would inject some much-needed funds, give the project fresh impetus, and of course there would have to be some changes. The first and most important of these concerned Héctor Roldán, who had quit the project because of his radical opposition to Mardanos.

"You don't say!" I said. "Was he thrown out?"

"No, he resigned."

"Goodness! So what happens now?"

"It's not a problem. There's no lack of candidates for director."

"I feel sorry for him. At his age . . . Who is this Mardanos?"

"Well, I have to admit he's not the associate I would have preferred," said Vilches. "But there was no time to find anyone else: the ministry's new grant system is going to take ages, and we desperately needed refinancing . . . Anyway, I'm sure you're not interested in the details. It's not serious. We've lost a director and gained a partner, that's all. What we should be grateful for is that Edgar Mardanos has deep pockets and is very well connected. For example, he went on at least fifty hunting parties with Franco."

"Good grief!"

"And he's enthusiastic about the project. He's going to propose another director, but he wants to talk to you first. He's very interested in getting to know you. He'll probably call you in a couple of days."

When I asked if he was still the one in charge at Vilma Films Inc., he answered in the coldest, most impersonal tone he could muster that the only thing that should interest me was that the arrival of a new producer meant that the film and everything I had written so far would not end up in the wastepaper basket. He added that Edgar Mardanos was very well known in film circles. He had produced more than a hundred films, including spaghetti westerns, spicy comedies and horror and science fiction movies. He had links to a powerful television channel about to break into the market, and had a substantial record as the author of erotic movies that had made a lot of money. He gave me some titles that made my hair stand on end: "Purita's Garter Belt", "Sister Guitar", "Spanish Striptease" and "Darling, What's My Best Friend Doing in Your Bed?"

Despite this, I tried to sound cheerful.

"Fantastic!"

"It's all above board," Vilches insisted. "Everything's under control, and we're determined to make a good film, right? So, in the meantime," he added in a slightly mocking tone, "try to learn a bit about how this business functions, my friend. Take the time to read the new cinema legislation, for example: that'll help you understand the balancing acts we have to perform. Well, I'll keep you informed."

Before hanging up, he reminded me once again exactly what I had been commissioned to do by Vilma Films Inc. This was a first treatment, not the actual screenplay, so whatever I might consider relevant – for example, whether or not the victim had been a police informant, was a whore by profession rather than out of necessity, or had turned her own husband over to the police, or if the murderer had committed the crime as a result of a shed-load of complexes for which he blamed his mother – none of that was more important than the random or simply inexplicable motives that led to the crime of passion. In other words, I should rein in my imagination and stick to the facts.

I said, fine, I would.

Three days later, I received a call from Edgardo Mardanos from his home in the wealthy Madrid neighbourhood of El Viso. In a relentlessly optimistic, singsong tone he told me he was dying to meet me, that he was very happy with my initial treatment of the film, and that he was thinking of coming to Barcelona as soon as possible to exchange thoughts.

He had a metallic, echoing voice that rang in my ears long after he had finished speaking. He told me that Roldán had left the production with a substantial payoff and was as happy as a sandboy. Vilma Films was looking at several names to replace him.

"Whoever they choose, it would be good to know as soon as possible," I said. "Roldán told me he didn't want a plot, but who knows if the new director—"

"Of course, of course," Mardanos cut in. "I'm well aware of what our dear friend Héctor didn't want. Let's just say that he wasn't interested in filming the asphyxiation of a prostitute, but rather the moral and political asphyxiation of that Spain, the Spain back then. Some ambition! Well, you can forget the strict docudrama that Roldán was proposing. Don't get me wrong: I've got a lot of respect for Héctor, but his insistence on reducing the whole film to a brilliant idea . . . I'm sure you'll agree with me that it's only geniuses who can manage that. Anyway, you're not mistaken, what we need now is for all of us to be pulling in the same direction. But we're on the right track, I'm sure of it!"

He added that what he had read of the treatment so far seemed to him excellent, though there were some supporting characters that he thought could be used to beef up the central theme.

"That Encarnita, for example." His voice became euphoric. "You've struck gold there! A sightless sex worker!"

"You mean the blind whore?"

"Of course! That poor girl dreaming of getting a guide dog!"

"So you think that—"

"Of course! She's a real find! You ought to make more of her. Seriously, it's a fabulous touch. A blind whore!"

"According to Sicart, she was a bit myopic, that's all. She had glaucoma and had lost twenty per cent of her vision, but wasn't completely blind."

"Well, she ought to be. Entirely blind, that is. Do you know something? Someone like that's never appeared before in the cinema, it's absolutely original. You can imagine her at work, doing everything blindly . . . in other words, working entirely by touch. That's the attraction, don't you see? A good actress could do wonders with a part like that. How come you didn't see it? You need to develop that character more, it's crying out for it! The film could be a box office hit! Who wouldn't want to see a blind sex worker in action?"

It occurred to me that our associate producer was already thinking about how to promote the film, of the publicity strategy, and that was why he preferred to speak of Encarnita as a sex worker or sex professional, rather than as a blind whore.

"I'm sorry, but it won't work," I said. "As far as I know, nowhere in the world has there ever been a blind whore. It won't wash."

"But you can make it work. You're a great writer."

"No, I'm not. And even if I were, I couldn't make something believable out of something that so clearly isn't."

"Don't tell me that, my friend. With a little bit of talent, you can sort that out."

He was right. All it was needed was the right actress, saucy dialogue and an unscrupulous director. Who on earth was bothered whether it rang true or not? He added that there was no need for the character to bring anything relevant or decisive to the film. It would be enough to see her in action, struggling with her visual handicap in a few scenes that would doubtless be very celebrated and commented on, if they were shot tactfully and tastefully, without overstepping the mark. His instinct told him that we were on to something original, entertaining and moving, a sure-fire formula for success. In other words, he saw Encarnita as one of those supporting roles that end up stealing the best scenes from the main protagonists.

"And as for it not being believable because it doesn't ring true . . ." His voice was filled with a metallic echo once more. "Listen, I'll tell you something funny. Do you remember Frank Capra's 'It's a Wonderful Life'? Well, that's a good film full of incredible elements. And the most incredible thing isn't that elderly guardian angel who has to earn his wings by a good deed, no sir: the most incredible thing is that the protagonist is attracted to Donna Reed when he has Gloria Grahame so close at hand! Ha ha ha!"

"Is that a joke?"

"I don't know, but it's as real as life! Ha ha ha. True to life." He calmed down gradually. "Well, we can talk more about that blind little whore, but I advise you to keep her in mind. And now I think about it . . . I've got the perfect actress for the role! Just so long as you give the character more relevance, of course. She's a promising young actress who needs a break. In fact, at this very moment she's acting in a theatre in Barcelona, you could go and see her."

I immediately made my excuses, claiming that unfortunately I had been forced to give up on the theatre due to an increasing deafness that prevented me enjoying the dialogue even if I was in the front row, which wasn't a complete lie. But Edgardo Mardanos was very keen for me to meet the actress. He said he would talk to her and that she would be delighted to pay me a visit, if that was alright by me. He added that the young actress's name was Elsa Loris, and that she had a great future ahead of her.

I said that was fine and continued to sound cheerful. We said farewell, exchanging best wishes. I hung up and in less than five minutes I'd forgotten all about it.

27. STREET OUTSIDE DELICIAS CINEMA, 1949. DAY. FADING DAYLIGHT.

Camera moves erratically at pavement level as it follows a trail of dirty water flowing down the gutter towards a drain where a rat's tail scuttles away, then on to the feet of a boy walking along and, finally, with obvious difficulties to focus the shot, it settles on the satiny silhouette of Gilda high outside the Delicias cinema at the end of the street.

(This is a visual metaphor for the difficulties of focusing on the main theme: the boy's feet are constantly moving out of shot. He is wearing scruffy boots and threadbare socks down round his ankles. Another boy wearing a raincoat runs after him and puts an arm round his shoulders. Laughing, they shadow-box. They are the same boys as in Sequence 5, but two years later.)

BOY 2: What do you bet we get in this time? We're not kids anymore, they have to let us in.

BOY 1: What do you mean, *nano*? Didn't you see the poster? Film prohibited for under fifteens. But we don't give a shit about that, do we?

BOY 2: I want to see the flyer, don't you? We'll ask the woman in the box office for one, then slip in.

Bright green blades of grass peep through cracks in the right-hand pavement going down the street. On the left at the corner with Calle Sant Luis, two men in berets and slippers come staggering drunk out of a tavern, arms linked round each other's shoulders. In the drizzling rain, they zigzag down the street, come to a halt and then turn around, head back up again, appear finally to get their bearings and lurch and stumble along the apparently deserted street towards

Travessera de Gràcia and the yellowing facade of the Delicias cinema, whose crudely painted billboards emerge out of the grey mist like a brightly coloured ship's figurehead. To the left of the cinema, beyond the entrance to the Popular Baths and the Catalonia Swimming Club, shine the lights of a corner bar.

CUT to interior of the bar. Ramón Mir is seated at a rear table with a plate of patatas bravas and a glass of wine. He loosens his belt and sits staring thoughtfully into space as he cleans his teeth with a toothpick. A shoeshine boy kneels in front of him to clean his boots.

CUT to the two boys standing on the pavement in front of the poster advertising "Gilda". They are admiring the star's satiny thighs, elbow-length gloves and golden mane of hair enveloped in the curling smoke from the cigarette. Their gaze pans up the front of the cinema to the projection booth skylight, where the face of a beautiful woman appears, cigarette between her lips. It's Carol, with dishevelled hair, sleepy eyes and lipstick smeared round her mouth. She shakes her head, pokes her bare arms out and seems to be testing the air with her hands.

Rooted to the pavement, the boys glance at one another expectantly. Carol throws down to them the strips of film she has picked up from the floor of the booth, and the two boys push and shove each other to catch them in the air. Boy 1 snatches a strip and holds the images up to the light.

BOY 2: Is it her? Let's see . . . Is she showing anything . . .?

CUT to Carol hanging out of the skylight. She is holding a cage with a budgerigar in it, its wings flapping frantically. She opens the cage door and the bird flies off into the overcast sky. Watching it disappear, she drops the cage, which smashes on the pavement outside the entrance to the cinema, close to the two boys, who are still peering at the lengths of film.

Carol remains at the skylight, smoking, eyes closed as she breathes in the damp street air. Her face looks calm and peaceful. Every so often her lipstick-smeared mouth blows out smoke rings that the drizzle immediately disperses. She throws away the cigarette, casts a quick, sad glance at the boys still fighting over the strips of film down below, runs her fingers through her hair and pulls her head back in.

CUT to the cinema box office, inside which the cashier has her head down, concentrating on her knitting. With a sigh, she watches the boys approaching, carries on with her knitting and says wearily:

CASHIER: You can't go in. It's for adults only.

BOY 2: We know that, Señora Anita. We only want programmes.

CASHIER: I've run out. I can give you next week's.

BOY 2: No, we want this week's. It's for my cousin Rosita. She collects them.

CASHIER (*smiling*): Yeah, yeah. Tell me, aren't you ashamed of yourselves? What are you hoping to see in the film? Good

Lord! And you, Lucas, who seemed like such a good boy. Do you want your mother to find out?

BOY 1: My mother says there's never been a woman like Gilda. Give me a programme, please.

CASHIER: I've already told you, I don't have any left. Come on, go home now, it's coming on to rain.

BOY 1: Shit! (*Pushes his friend*) Let's go!

They move away from the box office and stand looking at the entrance to the stalls, covered in a big red plush curtain. Sitting on a chair, head bowed, the usher is chatting to Ramón Mir, who has just arrived and stands listening to him, looking bored and still cleaning his teeth with a toothpick.

BOY 2: What shall we do, eh? Sneak in?

BOY 1: Not now. Can't you see the Fascist with the imperial turkeys on his shirt at the entrance? When he's gone and the usher starts reading the newspaper, that's when we'll have a chance.

11

I had just finished having lunch in the kitchen and Felisa was about to serve coffee when Sicart arrived unannounced. He apologised for coming early: he had a dentist appointment at half past five. He had toothache and had taken an Optalidon, which had had a strange effect on him, he said.

"Sometimes I think I've lost my marbles. I had to stop on my way here: I had no idea what street I was on."

"Did you get lost?" Felisa said.

"No, not at all! I was simply in a bit of a daze."

I told him to sit at the table and Felisa offered him a coffee.

"Could I have some ice in it?" he said, and added jokingly, "If it's not too much trouble, Señora Eloíiiisa."

Felisa glanced over her shoulder at him.

"Ice? No way! Do you want to wake up that tooth of yours, you ninny?"

"Fine, fine, I didn't say a word."

"And be very careful with the sugar. Just a pinch."

"Alright, just a pinch, señora," he said, winking at me.

He appeared to be in a good mood, wanting to have fun with her. He took out of his pocket a crude fan with a brightly coloured design I didn't recognise at first. He smiled slyly at me and began to fan himself. Felisa poured a meagre half spoonful of sugar into his cup and then placed the bowl out of his reach. She was performing. Coming and going from the dishwasher as she cleared the table, her languid fish eyes fell reprovingly on the drawing on the fan: the face of a clown sticking out his tongue.

Fanning himself with a slight smile, Sicart looked at me and said:

"A bit of fun never goes amiss, does it?"

For the first time I sensed he was properly at ease. Apparently the informal atmosphere in the kitchen, Felisa's sallies and jokes, her familiarity with me and the same carefree way she talked to him helped him relax and encouraged him to talk more freely. All of which led me to believe it would be the perfect moment to bring up the crime and its details, however sordid they might be.

"Would you like a drink, Sicart?"

"Not just now, thanks."

"Last night I read what the press said about what happened. You should see the nonsense they printed back then because of the censorship! It seems that Carolina Bruil wasn't a prostitute, or even a slut. She was a fallen woman, a woman of doubtful morals, of loose customs, a courtesan, even, a mistress. Although the latter was usually reserved for the very high-class, distinguished mistresses of the rich industrialists with a box at the Liceo opera house. Well, no newspaper could escape censorship in those days. And my goodness, the way they described the event, what they imagined happened in the projectionist's booth. Did you read it? You wouldn't agree with any of it, of course . . ."

I waited to see if this would get him started, but it didn't. A short while later I tried again.

"I've also read that it was raining heavily that day. Do you remember that?"

"Yes, I think I do." He closed his eyes and went on: "Yes, because when I saw her on the floor, with the length of film round her neck and her raincoat open, I put on my own coat . . . The number of times I've asked myself why on earth I did that, inside the cinema. I suppose I was thinking of going out into the street, of escaping, but I did neither . . . They said I went and sat in the back row of the stalls and didn't move until the police arrived, but I don't recall any of that."

"Well, at that moment you weren't in control of your actions."

"Wasn't I? And yet before I left, I focused the projector. I had heard the stamping and whistling from the stalls, so I decided to adjust it before I went out, so I can't have been that deranged."

"I understand. Then, after you had been sitting in the stalls for a while, the film got stuck again, didn't it? And there was nobody in the booth apart from Carol, and she was dead. Do you remember what she was wearing?"

"She was wearing a grey beret. My new assistant hadn't arrived yet . . . We were on to the third reel, if I'm not mistaken."

"Shall we talk about that now?"

"Now? No, I don't think so." He adjusted his glasses on his nose, stirred the coffee vigorously, almost violently, and added, without noticing the incongruence:

"No, today the weather's fine."

He gulped down his coffee. Another silence. I decided to try another tack, and so asked him more casually:

"What good films you could see in local cinemas in those days, couldn't you? By the way, the movie being shown at the Delicias that day was one of those that make history, wasn't it? You may have forgotten what it was . . ."

"Of course I haven't. It was 'Gilda'. What I don't remember is the other one, the B film, which must have been Spanish. I seem to remember it was 'Flower in the Shadows', but I'm not sure."

"'Gilda' had already been on many months earlier, more or less at the time you first invited Carol there, hadn't it?"

"Yes, that's true."

"Isn't that odd? It was still being shown a year and a half later?"

"No, that's not it," Sicart explained patiently. "It was brought back, and not once but many times. 'Gilda' was a huge success, everyone was talking about it. Listen, I know the film quite well. I loved it. I remember one particular scene because . . ." He looked across at me thoughtfully. "Have you seen it? It takes place in a cabaret. The audience applauds her after hearing her sing a song, and she's very happy and wild. She's a bit drunk, and starts to undo the zip of her dress, and asks someone to help her. And right at that point, the film catches fire. I can still hear the whistles from the stalls, but it wasn't my fault. The distributors often sent local cinemas films that were in tatters; sometimes they'd been spliced together so often they fell to pieces, and you had to make do as best you could. I repaired the reel quickly, but I had to chop out quite a long piece."

"Did that happen the first time it was shown, or the second, two years later?"

"It must have been when it was brought back. The film was in shreds."

There was an enormous rattling noise from the dishwasher, and it suddenly stopped. Felisa gave it a kick and it started up again. She came over to us, wiping her hands forcefully on her apron as though to settle things once and for all, whatever they might be, and said to Sicart:

"I bet you don't know what was said about that movie? Because it's true, I still recall that there was a lot of talk about 'Gilda', and it was because of something I'm sure you've forgotten, like so many other things."

Sicart looked at her, both confused and expectant.

"But I never . . . What do you mean?"

Felisa leant against the sink and took a cigarette out of the packet she always kept in her apron pocket. As she lit it, she glanced briefly at me for permission, smiling slyly.

"Can I tell you a good story?" she began, hidden behind a thick, very practised spiral of smoke. "Because it seems to me neither of you has heard what used to happen here in Spain. You see, with the censorship there was, whenever you went to the cinema to see a foreign film that was a bit let's say daring, you couldn't help but think someone had cut out the scenes in bed, or kisses they thought were too passionate. That's why a lot of people imagined things that were never there. Rumours went round about film stars in the nude when in reality they never had been, raunchy scenes supposedly suppressed by the censorship when the truth is they never existed . . ." Smiling, she gave us both a pitying smile. "Oh, those poor little Spaniards in the post-war years, who were dying to catch a glimpse of what the Catalans call *pit y cuixa*. So much so that the collective memory got to work and the funniest false rumour was spread about that film 'Gilda'. People said the censors had cut out a scene where Rita Hayworth stripped completely naked. That she performed a striptease. I'm sure you both remember, it starts with her taking off a glove while she's singing."

Sicart cleared his throat.

"Yes, of course I remember. Those were the fantasies of horny people, Señora Felisa. It's true there were lots of idiots willing to believe it, but there was nothing like that in the film. She didn't strip, I can assure you."

"That's right," Felisa said. "But what you apparently don't know, Señor Sicart, is that in 'Gilda' there's another scene where she does strip off."

Goodness, I said to myself, so our indomitable Felisa also has her version of that famous misunderstanding. I had a vague memory of that stale rumour going round the neighbourhood in the far-off days when I was fifteen, when the film was first shown at the Coliseum cinema and the grown-ups talked about it in the Comolada bar and in Frías's barber shop. As Felisa retold it, the story might simply have been another of her cinema buff's traps, but be that as it may, it was awakening Sicart's sleeping memory, and so I allowed her to carry on demonstrating her stupid cinematic expertise, and even encouraged her:

"Apparently our dear Felisa here has a big surprise for us," I said to Sicart. "And I bet I know what it is. It's what people said at the time: that the length of film around poor Carolina Bruil's neck when they discovered her dead body contained the famous striptease by Gilda that everyone was talking about, but which nobody had seen, because the censors ordered it be cut out."

"Is that what they said?" Sicart said, an incredulous expression on his face. He seemed to be about to burst out laughing. "My God, I'm sorry, but you have to be pretty stupid to think that we censored films in the projection booth, cutting out a piece here, a piece there . . ."

The dishwasher started to sneeze, stopped for a few moments, then started up again.

"I never said anything of the sort," Felisa said. "What I reckon is that there was a nude scene in the film and it was cut, and that it didn't take place in the casino, as people thought, but on a beach and at night."

"Good grief!" cried Sicart, still fanning himself. "This is getting complicated!"

"Don't be so annoying, Felisa, please," I said, conciliatory and provocative at the same time. "Are you trying to have us believe that, forty years ago, people were silly enough to swallow that story of a striptease?"

"And many other even more ridiculous things as well, I can tell you. I don't know why you're so surprised."

The dishwasher sneezed again.

"They have to come and repair it."

"Look here, Señora Clarisa," Sicart protested, "I agree my memory may be full of holes, but I'd bet an arm and a leg that in 'Gilda' there's no beach scene."

"Obviously not. Because it was cut out."

Felisa insisted that even the dumbest spectator must have realised the scene had been cut, because it was the second time that the girl had confessed she'd been to the beach for a swim in the middle of the night, talking about it in a very suggestive, provocative and sexy way. She described the moment in the film:

"It's when she's flirting in the casino at five in the morning, sitting on a gaming table with her guitar. She's been rehearsing a song and the man appears and asks her what she's doing there at that time of the morning, and where she's been. She replies: 'I've been swimming,' but he doesn't believe her, and asks: 'Oh yes, so where's your swimsuit?' And she gives him a provocative smile and says: 'It's under my dress. Would you like to see it?' and starts to lift her skirt—"

"So what?" Sicart interrupted, intrigued and amused despite himself.

"Well, good Lord, it couldn't be clearer, could it?" Felisa snorted. "That was the real nude scene we never saw because it was censored! But you couldn't know that, Señor Sicart, even though you were showing the film, because it was cut higher up the line!"

Sicart looked at me in astonishment. He took his glasses off and began to wipe them, stiffly. The noise from the dishwasher at the far end of the kitchen became louder and louder. I laid my hand on Sicart's shoulder to pacify him.

"Felisa means that the scene wasn't in the length of film round the neck of poor Carol because the censors had already got rid of it, before the film was distributed."

"Look here," Sicart muttered, "right now I couldn't tell you what was in those frames I chopped out, whether it was a beach or the sheikh of Araby, but I'd swear there was no woman in the buff. The film caught fire, and before I could glue it together with acetone and put it in the splicer, I had to cut out quite a lot – something that rarely happened to me, by the way. I remember that the leftover strip was lying on the floor, and that she picked it up, said, 'What a lovely corkscrew you've made,' and then wrapped it round her neck laughing, as if it was a necklace . . ." All of a sudden he stopped speaking, not wanting to continue in that direction. "Shit, all this is very strange. Besides, it's impossible, that piece of film can't have been a metre long. Do you know how many metres of film would be in a scene like the one you're describing?"

Felisa looked at him poker-faced, her attention apparently focused on the dishwasher's increasingly accelerated thumping.

"That thing is making the devil of a noise, Felisa," I said. "Aren't they supposed to come and fix it?"

"Tomorrow without fail," she said. Then, turning to Sicart: "You're right, Señor Sicart, there's something not quite straight in all this." Raising her forefinger, she added: "But don't let it get you down. I bet you don't know why the Chinese never use this finger, do you?"

"You're asking me? I haven't a clue."

"Because it's mine, ha ha ha. You're not very on the ball today, Señor Sicart."

"That's enough, Felisa," I said interrupting her once more. Patting Sicart on the back, I got up from the table. "Are you sure you don't want something to drink?"

"Listen." It was Felisa yet again. "Do you want to win some easy money in two shakes?"

"No, don't start on that," I said. "Anyway, there's no time. Señor Sicart has to go to the dentist. We'll work for a while on the terrace, so bring me a whisky and water, please."

"Right away." She stubbed the cigarette out in the sink and took a deep breath. "But both of you, listen carefully. We're up a mountain. A hunter aims his rifle at a deer. The deer stares at him, waits. The hunter fires into the air and says to the deer: 'Alright?'" She paused for effect, her eyelid drooping slowly and mischievously over her mocking eye. "So, who is the hunter that spares the deer's life? There's five pesetas in it for you if you get it right, Señor Sicart. If you don't, I'll accept your modest contribution to my meagre savings."

Sicart had also stood up.

"I haven't the foggiest idea," he said. He looked at me, his expression somewhere between confused and amused. "What about you?"

"Me neither." I took him by the arm and we left the kitchen. "And let me give you some friendly advice. Never, ever bet a single peseta with that woman if you don't want to see yourself robbed blind."

"What a killjoy," Felisa said, turning her back on us to attend to the wheezing dishwasher. "It's not right for you to slander me like that, it's not right. And now do me the favour of getting out of here, I have to tidy all this up."

12

By mid-July I already had sufficient information about the victim and her killer in the days leading up to the crime, but couldn't see what interest there might be in the detailed account of what two people did as they struggled along in such a predictable, dull manner: Carolina Bruil meeting the regulars at Panam's afternoon and evening, or taking on extra work arranged by Mir to please his colleagues, obscure officials in police stations or the Civil Government; drinking more than she should and fatally resigned to her sexual routine, to apathy and loneliness, waking up every day clutching her desperate bitterness and her bottle in a cheap boarding house on Calle Verdi, where the Falangist used to come and rouse her at mid-day; and Fermín Sicart in the Delicias projection booth, getting through a working day similar to hers, from four in the after-noon to midnight; in the morning helping his mother with the shopping or the housework in their dark little flat on Calle

San Ramón, at weekends playing cards with three neighbours in the backroom of a shop selling prophylactics and enemas near his home, or wandering round the neighbourhood taverns and brothels, where he was always well received, and being friendly and attentive towards his old colleague Liberto Augé. That man's relationship with Sicart's mother was of particular interest to me.

"I've got a couple of questions concerning your mother and Augé."

We had just settled on the terrace, and I had switched on the tape recorder. Sicart stood up with the chair sticking to his backside, and moved back a little to avoid having the sun in his face, while I changed the angle of the parasol to make sure he was in the shade. During our last session I had noticed that when Señor Augé came up in our conversation something happened to Sicart's voice: the tone changed, and he sounded unsure of himself.

"First and foremost, how come a libertarian like Augé, an anarchist from the Durruti Column no less, allowed you to call him Señor? Did your mother use that formal address as well?"

Sicart took off his glasses, hung them from the neck of his shirt, and fished the cigarette case out of his pocket. It took him several moments to respond, holding the case in his hands as though deciphering something on the lid.

"I always felt respect for him, and my mother always addressed him formally."

"But Augé and your mother were very close, weren't they?"

"Yes, or rather no . . . well, I'm not sure . . . it was so many years ago now. Yes, he wanted to help her." He twirled the cigarette case round and round in his hands, searching for the words. "He helped us at a very difficult time, but she repaid him very badly for it. All I can say is that I had a lot of respect for the old man. He used to talk to me about the trade union struggle, about his friends in the profession; he wanted me to give up whoring and join the union, he would say that we workers had to win our freedom, the future and our dignity, nonsense like that. I couldn't give a stuff about any of it, so sometimes we argued, but I never lacked respect for him. I didn't want to know anything about politics, although occasionally I would help him with his rounds because to me he looked so ill, and because he was my work colleague. Between the reels he would give me *Solidaridad Obrera* to read. I can still remember a slogan that always appeared in the newsletter: 'There's little distance between an indiscretion and a secret; it's our duty to block the agitator's way.' The fact is that I couldn't give a fig about all that, but, as I say, I always knew to show respect for older people. Above all to Señor Augé, who taught me the trade. I was his apprentice."

"I see. How long had he and your mother known each other?"

"I really don't know. He used to turn up at home." Taking a cigarette out of the case, he stared at it as if he didn't know what to do with it. "Back then I was a lout, a good-for-nothing, a trouble-maker and whoremonger. It was Señor Augé who took me off the streets. He educated me, and recommended me as a bicycle messenger boy. That was my first proper job." A lively gleam came into his eyes as he continued: "I used to be on the bike pedalling for all I was worth from one cinema to another with the reels in a sack."

Pausing to light the cigarette, he carried on, by now well ensconced in a memory that no doubt was enjoyable for him. There was a touch of pride when he talked of his apprenticeship alongside Señor Augé. He explained that when he was fifteen he had begun to work for a company that owned several cinemas that all showed the same film, but at different times: since they only had a single copy, when the first reel had finished in one cinema and the second reel was being shown, he would take the first one on his bike to the next cinema, and so on with all the remaining reels. He carried the cans on his back. The chief projectionist at the Padró cinema was Señor Augé, who was very well respected in the profession. He earned three hundred and fifty pesetas a week, and Sicart learned the trade alongside him, watching him work.

"I understand." I consulted my notes. "Let's see. You were born on 3 January 1920. In Barcelona's Chinese quarter."

"Yes."

"The son of a single mother."

Sicart felt for the glasses in his shirt pocket, wiped them

with a handkerchief, put them on, and looked at me. I could have sworn he was thinking "I know where you're headed". But what he said was:

"Yes, that's right."

"This isn't important, of course, but it could be useful as regards the screenplay. It seems as though your mother, Margarita Sicart, was very popular in the neighbourhood. They called her . . ." I searched once more in my notes. "Well, she had a funny nickname, although I guess you didn't think it was . . ."

Sicart shook his head wearily. Taking off his glasses again, he said:

"Rita the Sucker." His face contorted as he said: "And I couldn't give a damn about it, you know?"

"O.K. Why was she called that?"

"No idea. She used to like to drink barley water with a straw. It must have been because of that."

The line of shadow had moved up his face and the sun was hurting his eyes, but he didn't protect them with his glasses. I stood up to adjust the parasol again, and his face was once more submerged in shadow and in that fateful impassivity given it by having to confront such a sinister, disturbing past.

"It appears that as a kid you used to fight with anyone and everyone," I said. "Especially those who called your mother by that nickname."

"No, that's not right, it wasn't because of that. The thing is, I was always getting into scrapes."

"I understand. What can you tell me about your father?"

"Nothing. I haven't the faintest idea about that."

"Do you mean you don't know who he was?"

"No."

"Didn't your mother ever talk about him?"

"No, she never wanted to tell me anything . . ."

He fell silent when he saw Felisa coming out. She was bringing his beer, a plate of salted almonds and a whisky that was almost entirely water for me. After more than taking her time, she stood by the parasol, hands folded in front of her apron, staring at us.

"Do you want anything else?" she said eventually.

"Nothing, Felisa. Thank you."

She pottered about nearby, around the bush with the trumpet flowers, removing the withered blooms with her gloved hand. All of a sudden, the sun went in, and the evening grew dark with clouds.

Sicart rubbed his eyes, as if he was confused.

"I've forgotten what I was saying."

"That doesn't matter," I said. "Let's see. On the day of your last meeting with Carolina Bruil, the day of the crime, you were still living with your mother in the Chinese quarter. Your mother was young then, about forty years old . . ."

"Forty-three. She always took off three."

"What work did she do?"

"She worked as a seamstress," he said drily. "She could sew anything, she could stitch up holes in stockings and all that kind of thing, she had nimble fingers . . . But she had nothing to do with the Carol business. She died while I was in prison."

He seemed uneasy at the direction my questions were taking. I consulted my notes again, and went on:

"The case files include the testimony of an old friend of your mother's, someone called Rosita Márquez, who had run a brothel on Calle Robador, and who was a witness in your defence. She says that as a young woman of twenty-two your mother used to be a cleaner in that brothel, and—"

"I know nothing about that," Sicart cut in quickly, crushing his cigarette in the ashtray. "Look, this is something that gets up my nose, to put it mildly. Because that wasn't a brothel, no way, it was a workshop or dressmaking school, and it was there that my mother learned to sew. It was called El Recreo, that was where the confusion lay."

"I understand."

I didn't insist, because there was no confusion to clear up. At a certain period, El Recreo had been one of the three most popular and lively brothels on Calle Robador – the other two were El Jardín and La Maña, if I'm not mistaken – and the clumsy whitewash Sicart was offering me now, doubtless in the belief that the name would mean nothing to me, could only confirm what I had seen in the files: at the age of twenty,

Margarita Sicart was employed in a brothel in the Chinese quarter as a cleaner and every so often a seamstress. It was at that time that she met Liberto Augé, who sublet a flat in the building opposite, worked as the assistant to a portrait photographer on the Rambla, and was taking a short course to qualify as a projectionist. At the age of thirteen, Sicart was messenger boy for a chemist on Calle Hospital, and on the side sold cosmetics, creams and potions to the neighbourhood whores. He spent the whole day out on the street up to no good, until two years later Señor Augé offered him his first proper job. The projectionists were already part of the C.N.T., and had established their personnel and wages with the distributors, thanks above all to the combative union activity of Señor Augé and his colleagues.

"Shortly after the war, when Señor Augé was already the chief operator at the Padró cinema," Sicart said again, "he recommended me to the owners, and I began work as a bicycle courier. I was fifteen. They gave me a bike, and I took sacks with the reels in them from one cinema to another. As well as the Padró, they owned the Bohemia, and the two cinemas both used the same copy, but at different times; once the Padró had shown the first two reels, I would pedal as fast as I could to take them to the Bohemia; then I would have to take the other reels without being a minute late. It was a tough job when it rained, and very serious, with a lot of responsibility. The pay wasn't bad, but Señor Augé used to say that the cyclist should be considered an assistant operator, and in his free time he taught me what to do. The fact is, he behaved like a real father towards me."

"According to your statement, Señor Augé was a good friend to your mother. Or was he something more than that?"

"Well, I think he loved her . . . in his own way. He used to come to the flat a lot." He was thoughtful for a while, then added: "I wish there had been something more between them because, you know, he was a good man, an upright sort. But my mother didn't want to know, she never listened to him, she was stubborn as a mule. She ignored him, laughed at his advice, provoked him. Then one day she was so spiteful he couldn't take it anymore. That was what happened, and it was a real shame." Sicart fell silent for a moment, then said: "You may not believe it, but my mother could have lived much better, but she refused, she insisted on carrying on working! So she would go to yet another damned dressmaking school and ruin her health with all the extra hours she put in, day and night. Señor Augé was very worried about her; he asked her on several occasions to stop. He wanted to recommend her for the job of ticket seller in one of the company's cinemas. A less stressful job. But my mother refused point blank, and in the end sent him packing. Can you understand it?"

"Why do you think she behaved so unkindly towards such a good man?"

Sicart took a deep breath.

"She never really appreciated him. It's not for me to say, but when it came to him my mother was . . . well, I could have smacked her. Señor Augé wanted to help us, and she sent him rudely on his way. That was the biggest mistake of her life. From that day on, everything went downhill in our house."

He fell silent, staring down at the back of his hand as if he could read something there.

"I understand. Your mother preferred to go on working at . . . Let's see . . ." I leafed through my notebook, but could not find what I was looking for. "I thought I'd written it down. Did you say it was a dressmaking academy?"

Sicart hastily put his glasses back on.

"Yes, I think that's what it was called . . . Madame Petit's Dressmaking Academy."

This fine-sounding name did not appear in any of the trial records, but I recognised it, although not exactly in connection with the demands of domestic fashion.

"The thing is," Sicart said, "my mother never wanted to back down, she didn't want to stop working. He asked her a thousand times to leave, and that led to a lot of arguments, until one day Señor Augé's patience ran out, and he never visited us again."

I heard the tape recorder click and got up to turn the cassette over. As I was doing so, I saw Sicart spinning the cigarette case in his hands. All at once he stood up and apologised; he had to go to the bathroom. Adjusting his glasses on his nose, he re-assumed his retired psychopath's mask, impassive and distant. He began to walk very slowly across the terrace on his way to the living room, and when he passed Felisa, who was busy deadheading her favourite flowers, some parrot beak blooms hanging from a bucket next to the sink, he stopped to admire the luminous explosion of orange flowers with their red tips, fleshy and as bright as a flame. I suddenly recalled the day my assistant planted them beneath a dark sky with storm clouds gathering. She told me that a friend of hers, a horticultural expert, claimed that this flower was a wonder of the imagination in the plant world, a paean to man's dreams and secret desires, and called it the Flower of Fictions. And I recalled that this fantastic story about the exultant lotus flower was accompanied that day by a display of thunder and lightning that crowned with its flashes and crashing sounds one of Felisa's most memorable performances. Now, seeing Sicart standing next to these cascading flowers, staring at them as if trying to discover the secret of their dazzling colour, I associated that extraordinary Flower of Fictions with what sounded to me like an absurd cock and bull story: Madame Petit's Dressmaking Academy.

Felisa had interrupted her pruning and was looking at Sicart with a friendly smile, the secateurs at the ready in her hand.

"Are you on your way to Oz, Señor Sicart?"

"What's that . . . ?"

"If you're going to the toilet."

"Oh, yes I am."

"Follow the yellow brick road."

Half mocking and half resigned, Sicart grimaced at her, shrugged and went inside the house. I gave my assistant a warning look, but said nothing. Shortly afterwards, Sicart re-emerged and stood next to her once more. He pointed at the exuberant flowers.

"What did you say they were called? The flowers of Oz?"

"No, Señor Sicart, but it doesn't matter. You look very tired."

I thought the same, and before he sat down again I suggested we bring the session to a close. I offered him a last glass, but he refused, and nor did he want me to accompany him to the door. He extended his hand and said in a strangely subdued voice:

"Alright. Tomorrow I'll tell you how I did it."

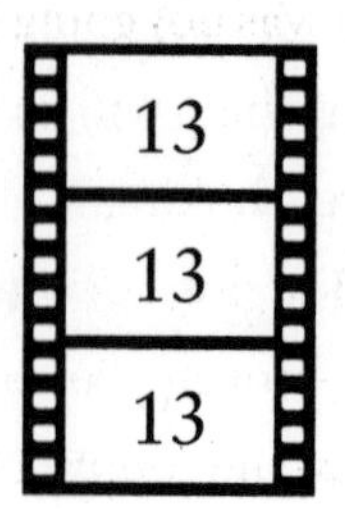

Madame Petit's Dressmaking Academy kept going round in my brain: the name had vaguely indecent, even hidden resonances. To resolve my doubts, I telephoned *La Vanguardia*, where an old journalist friend of mine worked.

"Dressmaking, did you say? Well, that depends on your point of view," said Luis with a laugh. "It was a brothel. It was on Calle Arc del Teatre, number six. Before the war it was one of the most select brothels in the Chinese quarter. It closed about thirty years ago."

"Fantastic!"

The following day Edgardo Mardanos called to inform me the new director of the film would probably be José Luis de Prada, someone he had suggested. He was a celebrated relic from the old Spanish cinema of long wigs and imperial flounces produced by the Cifesa company, once a highly thought-of professional who had survived this historical-patriotic garbage by reinventing himself for the current fashion of erotic movies and picaresque comedies. The news was not exactly promising, but I was not going to let it get me down.

"Splendid! Now everything will go smoothly, I'm sure."

"I know what you're thinking," Mardanos replied. "*Entre nous* I can tell you that I'm not a devotee of Prada's either. But no-one can deny he's a proven professional. You should bear that in mind. But anyway, the contract hasn't been signed yet."

"Whoever it is, it would be good to know what he wants from the film."

"Of course, we all have to pull together. But . . . is there a problem?"

"It's Sicart. He's keeping things from me." I had absolutely no wish to complicate things still further, but I couldn't help myself. "I'm discovering that he's a polyhedric personality. Everything he tells me suggests a case of paranoid schizophrenia, a psychological disturbance. His story reeks of it. That could be very fruitful, but it would be a different film, a docudrama with a very noir side to it."

I knew that behind the successful producer lay an unscrupulous rogue, and so I set out to tempt him with a truculent, madcap melodrama. I explained that Fermín Sicart, our protagonist caught up in the snares of memory, was hiding the fact that his mother had worked in a brothel, in other words, that she too was a prostitute, just like Carolina Bruil. This suggested to me very significant parallels, and paved the way for a passionate narrative closely linked to the crime, always provided of course that this subtle storyline was of interest to the new director.

"So the prostitute Carol," I concluded rashly, "could have been the mirror in which, that fateful day, Sicart saw the reflection of his mother, whom he hated for not having provided him with a father."

"My God, are you trying to sell me a motorbike, or what?" Mardanos said with a laugh.

"Well, yes, but we've seen worse rubbish in psychoanalytical films that, don't forget, have made lots of money. And it's not that far-fetched: Sicart is ashamed of his mother and conceals his past with clumsy lies, and yet he has no problem accepting his beloved whore and even boasts about his love-making prowess. That poorly assumed emotional contradiction could explain his crime, don't you think? The fact is, I'm discovering a character with endless secret compartments . . . In reality, what he doesn't remember could be much more interesting than what he does remember. It could work. I even have the title: 'The Mask and Amnesia'."

"So? Where is all this leading us?" asked Mardanos.

"To a more interesting character and a more complex story."

I mentioned too that there were reasons to think that Liberto Augé was bisexual or something close to it, and what was most important of all: that Fermín Sicart believed he was his natural son. From adolescence on, he felt or imagined that Augé was looking after him, and whenever he mentioned him, a kind of filial nostalgia surfaced, a respect and affection that went beyond friendship. What is more, I said, it was possible that Sicart was afraid he had been conceived by accident in a brothel, which would explain his efforts to try to find a father.

"With the result that our uncanny protagonist," I insisted self-importantly, "suspecting he might be the product of what you might call professional negligence, in other words the chance, unwanted fruit of a trick in a brothel that his mother saw as routine and against which she didn't take adequate precautions, attempted to rid himself of the ignominious fantasy of being fathered by someone who was nothing more than a passing client – something that ashamed and anguished him – by choosing as a father Señor Augé, an upright man who furthermore was so concerned about his mother that he wanted to take her out of the brothel and change her life . . . In other words, we could establish a relation of cause and effect by developing that tempting narrative storyline, if, I insist, that is of interest to the new director: the adolescent Sicart conceals his secret hatred of his mother for being a prostitute and above all for rejecting the father he wants, and that emotional knot could be at work in the adult Sicart's subconscious when he strangles Carol, apparently without realising what he is doing."

"All that is mere conjecture," Mardanos said. "In proper doses, it would be marvellous in a T.V. soap opera, in one dollop in a film it would be indigestible. There are starting to be too many whores and melodramatic queers in your story, don't you think? And too much psychodrama. No, look, I don't reckon that's the way we should go. I know this industry, so let me tell you something . . ."

"But I need to know what kind of film we're aiming for. Héctor Roldán wanted the crux of the drama to be the real human being, not the investigation of the crime. Is that where we are now: a fictional documentary, or what?"

"Listen, forget about experiments and tell a good story, with a narrative or a plot, or whatever you choose to call it."

"But that's not the same. And there's the problem. Who was it who said there are lots of ways to tell a story, but only one plot?"

"That's enough of your riddles! In my opinion, we need a radical rethink. We talked about it the other day, if you remember. Encarnita, my friend. We have Encarnita!"

I said nothing, and Mardanos followed up the point that really interested him: how was I getting on with the blind whore? Was that remarkable character gaining importance, creating room for itself, as he had suggested? Had I had the opportunity to meet Elsa Loris, that marvellous actress who would make the role hers?

"You ought to go and see her at the theatre," he insisted.

"You'd realise what potential she has, and that would encourage you to develop the character in your film. I'm sure of it. In one scene she appears naked, but only for a moment. Naturally, I'm not suggesting you should go and see her for that."

"No, of course not."

"Rather for her tremendous talent for making people laugh. She's sensational."

By now I had heard enough, so I brought the matter to a conclusion.

"Fine, ask her to come and see me. And please, keep me informed."

"Of course. And don't forget Encarnita!"

28. DELICIAS CINEMA, 1949. EXTERIOR/INTERIOR. DAY.

The camera pans slowly across the facade of the cinema covered in posters. Cigarette smoke curls round Rita Hayworth's face, smeared by a fine rain. A fantastical atmosphere engulfs the scene, as we hear the noise of the projector getting louder and louder. Peering out of the projection booth skylight, a cigarette in her mouth and still holding a birdcage, Carol follows with her gaze the bird that has just flown into the drizzling rain. The skinny, trembling hand with red-painted nails closes the empty cage. At first the bird hovers above the street, then flies high up into the clouds. When she sees it disappear, Carol drops the cage into the street.

INTERIOR OF THE PROJECTION BOOTH: Standing

barefoot on a chair, Carol closes the skylight, gets down and picks up a bottle of wine from the small table beside her. She drinks from it, then sits down, adjusting her black stocking and the garter on her thigh.

Alongside the projector, Sicart finishes focusing the film, wipes his hands on a rag and looks over at her with an annoyed but patient expression. There is an unlit cigarette in his mouth.

SICART: Why did you do that? You can't imagine what Señor Augé will say. He loves that bird.

CAROL (*a pleading look in her eyes*): We have to let it fly away. Please, please!

SICART: What's wrong with you? The fact is, it's not right.

CAROL: With all the noise in here, I don't know how the poor thing could bear it.

SICART: It got used to it. Señor Augé thinks it must be deaf. What am I to say to him?

CAROL (*smiling seductively*): There are some boys outside who begged me to set it free. And from the heavens Dani has just asked me the same. Don't you believe me?

SICART (*looking at her sadly*): Sweetheart, when are you going to stop using your boy as an excuse? And by the way, don't throw any more bits of film into the street; dammit, I've already been warned about that.

CAROL: Alright, but you mustn't light that cigarette either.

You know you can't smoke in here, it's dangerous.

SICART: It's just to anticipate the pleasure. Come on, come over here.

Carol picks up a corkscrew of film from under the table and drapes it round her neck. She unbuttons her blouse, undoes the zip on the side of her skirt, removes her top, takes another swig from the bottle and with slow, weary gestures finishes undressing. She adjusts the stockings and garters again and then pulls the raincoat round her shoulders and walks towards Sicart, eyes tight shut.

A close-up on Sicart smiling at her with the unlit cigarette dangling from his mouth. The whirring of the projector stops all of a sudden, and there's an ellipsis, and a flashback takes us to Sicart's adolescent face, fourteen years earlier, at the moment when the boy also strikes a match and, staring at us mischievously, is about to light a cigarette.

29. CHINESE QUARTER, 1935. EXTERIOR/DUSK.

The menacing face of the adolescent Sicart (aged 15), torn T-shirt, corduroy cap, loutish appearance) as he lights his butt end. He has a bloody lip and a split eyebrow.

SICART: You're a shit! I'm going to thrash you, kid.

Throwing away the cigarette, he charges at his opponent.

He's in the middle of the street fighting with two boys of a similar age to him. Punches and kicks. He has just cornered one of them in the doorway of a bar and is thumping him when a muscular hand grabs him by the throat and hauls him off his quarry.

It's Liberto Augé (aged 42, shaven head, blue overalls, espadrilles). He pushes him up against the wall and is about to reprimand him when all of a sudden a small cage crashes down on the pavement beside them. In it is a small budgerigar, miraculously unharmed.

Leaning over a first-floor balcony, Sicart's mother Margarita (aged 29, peroxide blonde, attractive) in a housecoat. Dishevelled hair, cigarette in mouth, she flings her arms about, screaming, and throws down a small, unfastened cardboard suitcase. Several items of clothing, an old raincoat, a pair of greasy gloves, and a cap fly out. As she is doing this, she is shouting:

MARGARITA: You can keep all this, Liberto, you bastard. I don't want anything of yours in my house! And don't come back! Go find yourself a bumboy to suck you off, you queer, you! Can you hear me, Liberto? I've had it up to here with you! Get out of my life! Get lost, will you!

His back against the wall, the adolescent Sicart watches as Liberto Augé listens to the insults without reacting, then bends down to the grimy cobbles and straightens the cage as best he can, with the little budgerigar cowering inside it. He recovers the raincoat and the cap, which is streaked with dirt. He stays crouching down for a while, head lowered, shaking the cap and slowly brushing it clean. He stands up and looks at the balcony (I suggest an aerial shot from above) then glances at the boy, ruffles his hair affectionately, turns on his heel and walks off down the street with the damaged cage in one hand and the raincoat over his shoulders.

(Commentary on this last shot, if it's of interest: Señor Augé, walking away with his suitcase and with his raincoat round his shoulders, destroys the boy's dream of seeing him united with his mother and prefigures the stiff, gloomy, marginal and vaguely dangerous image that the adult Fermín Sicart will adopt years later, with another old-fashioned raincoat round his shoulders. This is a formal device that brings together an ethical consideration and a fundamental metaphor: this "reflection", this play of mirrors between father and son, if I comment on it to Sicart and he thinks it's plausible or in some way decisive, could perhaps serve to clear away some of the cobwebs of his shattered emotional memory, and, who knows, might bring to light secrets that we could turn into storylines and subplots that would strengthen the narrative, make it more rounded, deeper, more interesting. This is only a suggestion.)

14

One stiflingly hot Monday, three days after the last call from the producer Mardanos, the promising young actress Elsa Loris appeared at my front door. I couldn't have cared less about her supposedly ideal attributes to play the blind whore, an episodic character I had barely sketched in, and so I resolved to cut short the visit and the topic, trying all the same not to offend her. But I had reckoned without Felisa.

That day I went for a swim earlier than usual, hoping to avoid Señora Falp, but when I got to the pool the first thing I saw was the lengthy trail of white foam left by the ancient woman's whirling feet as they thrashed through the water. She ploughed from one end to the other, demonstrating her powerful, impeccable backstroke, and as she turned she greeted me with her broad, toothless, pink and somehow touching smile. The three lanes were busy, so she waved for me to join her in hers. I dived in at the deep end, hoping to feel immediately anaesthetised by the strongly chlorinated water and its pungent hospital smell. As I swam, I started to write in my mind, staying underwater as long as possible, especially when I crossed with the thrashing swimmer. Writing is like holding your breath underwater, declared someone whose brilliant life was a shipwreck; it may be that I subscribed to that notion. But each time Señora Falp passed me, enveloping me in the whirlpool of bubbles left in her wake by her furious kicks, she succeeded in destroying my carefully constructed image of Carolina Bruil in the projection booth, the decisive image in the decisive scene, the one I had been trying for days to get right and was completely obsessed with: naked, with black (fishnet?) stockings, the raincoat round her shoulders and the strip of film round her neck, the unhappy prostitute approaches her killer with a smile on her face and with that strange request: "Hurry up . . ."

I recalled how, during one of our sessions, Sicart, exhausted and upset at the way I was insisting he give a precise description of a certain atmosphere and certain details, suddenly protested: "Hey, listen, don't I have the right to forget?" and all of a sudden there, underwater, as I recalled his protest, the feeling that I was wasting my feeble talent on contemptible, worthless rubbish led me to ask myself yet again: "Why don't you say to hell with it all, and dedicate yourself to your own work? Seeing that the question that really motivates and interests you – the failings of memory, dissembling, supplanted personalities, the refusal to accept guilt, playing a role – is of no importance whatsoever to the film's producer or director, why don't you just give up?" All the while, Señora Falp, propelling herself through the water with her powerful, smooth strokes, left behind swirls of turbulent water that made me lose track. I swam with my head underwater for as long as I could so as not to see or hear her, but when I surfaced, she had pulled up in front of me and was looking at me with a cheerful grin on her face.

"What's this? Why are you hiding?"

"I'm not . . ."

I took out one of my silicone earplugs to hear her better.

"What are you doing underwater all the time then?"

"Crosswords," I said, my mouth full of bubbles. "I find I can do them down there."

"The thing is, you give up too easily."

"But I'm not competing, Señora Falp. I'm happy simply to float."

"Well, it looks as if you're hiding!"

Her jubilant, toothless mouth was contorted in a grin; her ruby earring flashed its signals at me from beneath the surface. Why is this good lady making fun of me, I wondered. The next time she overtook me, the waves and clamour she made, together with the extraordinary profusion of bubbles produced by her flailing feet, enveloped me so violently that the earplug slipped out of my hand and disappeared in a spectacular cascade of water. As I put my face under to try to recover it, I noticed the water penetrating my outer ear like a stealthy caterpillar. Several times I caught sight of the feeble gleam from the ruby when the pink mermaid turned for another length, but there was no sign of the plug. Eventually, worried I might get otitis again, I clambered out of the pool.

When I reached home, Felisa was sitting in the kitchen going over the shopping list, already dressed to go out. I took a beer out of the fridge, went onto the terrace, and hung my swimming trunks, towel and cap on the clothes line. It can't have been more than ten o'clock, but the sun was already punishingly hot. I shut myself in the study, drew the blinds, and once more conjured up the phantom of Carolina Bruil in the deceptive darkness of the Delicias projection booth.

I began work. Scarcely ten minutes had gone by when Felisa came in carrying her shopping bag to ask whether I had anything to add to her list. Nothing, I said. As she was leaving, she paused in the doorway and turned back towards me.

"Oh, I almost forgot. A very pretty young lady who says she's an actress is here. She looks like . . . Well, do you remember 'Hot Lips'? I told her you were busy, and she's waiting for you out on the terrace."

Her offhand tone told me that for some reason or other she did not approve. I pulled back the blind and could see the young actress standing next to the unopened parasol, her buttocks pressed against the edge of the table, and a magazine over her head to protect her from the sun's rays. This young talent who needed a push was a tall, slender blonde with a kittenish face, short luxuriant hair and spectacular legs. She was wearing a white sleeveless blouse, denim miniskirt and designer sandals, and had a pair of purple-framed sunglasses pushed high up on her forehead. She was exactly what was to be expected from an eccentric, salacious producer like Mardanos; she not only revealed his personal tastes but also indicated what his next film would be like, how he saw it and wanted it to be: extravagant sunglasses, miniskirt, beautiful thighs and a pert behind. At first glance, I realised I had vaguely seen her somewhere: in some T.V. trash with a huge audience in Spain, one of those programmes with canned laughter, where with great self-assurance she played the role of a fresh-cheeked, unsqueamish nurse taking care of lusty elderly gentlemen in an old people's home. Garbage, but a big hit for the state broadcaster. It was obvious that Felisa had decided to leave her out on the terrace to fry in the sun without a hint of compassion, not even opening the parasol or bringing her so much as a glass of water.

"You could at least have offered her some sunscreen."

"Very funny," Felisa said. "She won't come to any harm, she's as fresh as a daisy. Or haven't you taken a good look at her yet? I've seen a lot of her, you know. Last week she was on that T.V. chat show, 'Baring Hearts', and the poor girl, well . . .

it was clear it wasn't exactly her heart she wanted to bare. Anyway, I'm off to the market. I'll be right back."

When I went out onto the terrace, Elsa Loris was trying unsuccessfully to open the parasol. She struggled wearily in the blinding sunlight; sweat was already running down her neckline.

"Señorita Loris, I presume," I said, extending my hand. "Leave that and follow me. We'll be better off inside."

"Pleased to meet you. Phew, that's a relief!" She had a moist, nasal, still childlike voice. "I hope I'm not interrupting your work, I know this isn't the best time, and with this heat. But Edgar told me you and I ought to meet, that it would be good for the film, and so . . . here you have me."

I got the odd impression that when she said 'Here you have me' her shiny, lipsticked lips protruded slightly in front of her splendid row of teeth, as though her mouth was sucking in air as she spoke; above it were her smiling cheeks with prominent cheekbones, her fine forehead and a nose that was just too snub for my liking. In the study she sat in an armchair with her back to the window, and her blonde curly hair shone against the light. She took the sunglasses out of her hair and from time to time raised one of their arms to her mouth. I could detect the fruits of Felisa's mean trick from the sweat still glistening in her plunging cleavage, and from the very first moment could think of nothing but how to cut short her visit. Even so, I will not deny that her juvenile pectoral attributes (to borrow a phrase from Pilar Rajola, that verbal acrobat from the favourite variety acts of my childhood) aroused a certain curiosity in me. There was something still innocent about the curls on her forehead that contrasted with the encroaching harsh lines of adulthood that surfaced whenever she smiled her lipstick-saturated smile.

"A Coca-Cola, but in a little while," she said. "That's really kind of you . . . I would have come late in the afternoon so as not to interrupt your work, but the two performances at the Victoria theatre don't leave me much time."

"I understand." I moved a couple of books from the other armchair and sat opposite her. "So you're the actress they're suggesting for the role of . . ."

"Encarnita, the main lead's friend. It was Edgar's idea. He's so enchanted with Encarnita! And so am I!"

"It's very flattering, but I don't think I have the power to—"

"Edgar says it will take only a word from you and the role will be mine. But not just that. Edgar is determined that Encarnita should be like me in a really cool way, and that you and I ought to meet. And since you haven't come to see me at the theatre, this morning I got up and said to myself, 'Off you go!' So here you have me. That's what I'm like!"

"So I see. But tell me, what play are you in?"

"'Witness for the Prosecution'. It's a new production, based more on the film than on the original play . . . You'd love it.

I'm Miss Plimsoll, Sir Wilfrid the barrister's nurse. In the film she was played by Elsa Lanchester, I don't know if you remember."

"Ah yes, Miss Plimsoll. An insufferable woman."

"Well, in this version she's quite different, you see."

She swallowed her *r*s and spoke slowly in a throaty, sweet way, as though spreading honey on her words. In fact, a fly that had just flown in through the window was already buzzing round her head. "The nurse wasn't in the original play, she appeared for the first time in the film. So my character comes from the cinema, not the theatre. And there are new scenes that are really funny which aren't exactly from the play or the film either, such as when I chase after Sir Wilfrid to get him to try on a pair of ghastly Bermudas I bought him for his holidays. And to encourage him I'm wearing a super-cool bikini."

"Fantastic!"

"It's an easy and very sympathetic character. But of course, Miss Plimsoll is nothing like your Encarnita. From what Edgar tells me, Encarnita is a professional. I mean, she gets straight on with it."

"Oh yes, of course." I sat for a while, unable to think of what to say next. "So Edgar Mardanos sees you as incarnating Encarnita . . . Sorry, I didn't mean that as a joke. What I meant to ask was . . . how do you see Encarnita? Oh look, there's a fly on your knee!"

There indeed was the fly, its little feet clinging to her silky, tanned skin, apparently very much at home. She didn't even look down at it.

"Well . . . I see her as an innocent, caring, cheerful . . . and very sexy woman! I'm a complete fan of Encarnita's!"

"But the thing is, to use the producer's elegant formula, she's a sex worker. And she's blind. Doesn't that seem extremely unlikely to you? Did you ever hear of a working blind prostitute? Do you really think that kind of work can be done . . . by touch, shall we say?"

"Of course! Why not?" Her hard, calculating smile flashed out once more. "Didn't you know that a lot of women do it blindly . . .? I'll tell you something: Encarnita is a well-rounded character! Edgar thinks she should have a much bigger role."

"It's not easy, you know." I stood up to look for the packet of cigarettes that must be somewhere on the desk among all the papers, but couldn't find it. "I've had a few ideas, but I'm not sure. What do you think of a scene where Encarnita has a client who's blind as well?"

"Oh! That's so cool!"

"She could have a pimp who provides her with unconventional clients, let's say with oddballs." I hesitated a second, sat on the edge of the untidy desk and carried on improvising: "A deaf and dumb man, a blind guy, a hunchback, maybe a dwarf. In fact, the pimp himself could be a bit of a zombie . . . Let's see, he's ugly and has a hump, right? Encarnita is a very extraordinary woman, isn't she? She's a Catholic, goes to Mass every

Sunday, and kneels and prays at the altar. She's a Roman Catholic whore, shall we say, and she wants to create a union with her fellow sex workers. Her greatest dream is to have a guide dog, a Labrador. She may not be able to read, but she has a heart of gold. She's never thought of it, and wouldn't be able to explain it, but she might well say: 'My body is also a temple of the Lord.' Are you following me, Señorita Loris?"

"Of course! Encarnita is experiencing a crisis of conscience!"

She raised her arms, showing the joyous, innocent curve of her armpits, then put both hands behind her head to straighten her hair. As she did so, a button on her blouse popped undone.

"No, it's not that," I objected perversely. "Her sightless eyes do not judge the urges or servitude of her naked body, and, careful now, nor does she judge the men who are slaves to their desires. Encarnita is not aware of being in any way transgressive, she has no notion of sin, right? But she has an astonishing tactile memory, she can remember bodies, lips, backs, buttocks, scars . . . If ever the kisses she receives, or the hands that caress her, contain or express the slightest token of affection, however clumsy or slight, she is wonderfully equipped to sense it and be grateful . . . When she fakes an orgasm, her eyes are tight shut and she can't of course see her client's look of thanks, but she keeps an emotional memory of it, right?" I fell silent for a moment, astounded by the complete garbage I was spouting. "And what do you reckon if, when she hears her friend Carol has been murdered, she decides to quit the profession, so that at the end of the film we see her happy and content selling lottery tickets in a Blind Society kiosk?"

"I think it's brilliant! I can see her clearly from start to finish, I can even see how she should move! Can I tell you something? I imagine Encarnita going about her work in an entirely new, groundbreaking way. I'd like to show you, if you've no objection . . ."

She stood up, adjusted her miniskirt, went to the study door, turned round and walked back with her eyes closed, deliberately slowly, chin raised, as if she were in a trance. I was still leaning against the edge of the desk. I had found the packet of Ducados and lit one. The future star of the silver screen came towards me rehearsing her blindness, fumbling her way along, passionate and beyond any doubt beautiful, measuring each step with her right hand out in front of her, as though searching for support. She seemed to want to touch the armchair to help guide herself and avoid stumbling before she reached the desk, but at the last moment she changed direction and her hand groped forward, briefly landing on my trouser front.

"Oh, I'm so sorry," she said. "I didn't mean to . . . But that's more or less what might happen to Encarnita, isn't it?"

"More or less, yes."

"I can do better. It's just to give you some idea of how I see myself acting as a blind woman. You haven't seen me do anything like that, have you? Did you see 'Chaos in Marbella 2'? I was quite good in that." She sat down, sighed and crossed and uncrossed her legs once or twice. "And there's something else: I know what kind of wardrobe Encarnita should have. Those poor girls wear emotional clothes. And I love wearing emotional clothes!"

Her lively chatter, the product of a spontaneous, inexplicable enthusiasm, kept me entertained for more than half an hour, until I decided enough was enough. Her pink-varnished fingers were playing with the loose button on her blouse without the slightest intention of doing it up, but nor, I think, of taking things any further. As far as I was concerned, the role of Encarnita was hers for the asking. When I told her so, she was delighted, and seemed even less inclined to leave. It was then I heard a creak from the study door and the sound of clinking cans. I deduced Felisa must be back from the market.

"Well, I for one am convinced. You can count on me," I said, considering the matter resolved and the interview at an end. "But I'm afraid all this is premature, and besides, I don't choose the cast . . ."

"Oh, that's so cool, I can hardly believe it!" she exclaimed. "I was so nervous coming here! Now I'd really like to have that drink, and I'd like you to toast to wish me luck. Will you? Do say you will!"

Jubilant, the future star smiled, shook her head and began frantically to stroke her thighs, as if trying to rub the skin off them. There was another sound, out in the corridor, and through the half-open door I caught sight of a shadow moving away.

When I entered the kitchen, Felisa was arranging the beers and tonic waters from her shopping in the fridge.

"Here, take her this." She passed me a can of tonic water. "And don't worry, I'll deal with her. It seems to me your mind is elsewhere today, so leave it to me."

"Were you listening at the door, Feli?"

"Me?"

"Yes, you. Can I know what you're up to? Hey look, this tonic is hot as hell."

I handed it back to her. Felisa took another one from the fridge and left it on the table. Then she went over to the sink and started to wash lettuce leaves under the tap, while I opened myself a beer. I was about to leave the kitchen when I heard her say:

"I'm not going to allow that rosebud in there to make us late for lunch."

I went back to the study with the drinks, but before going in I paused in the doorway for a moment to get a good look at Elsa Loris without her seeing me. She was sitting in the armchair with her legs drawn up, arms round them and her chin on her knees, eyes closed. Curled up tight in some dream or other, she had shed her put-on look of a budding slut and appeared to me like a vulnerable, needy little girl. So I went in prepared to be friendly, and toasted the young actress for all her wishes to come true, even though by now I couldn't wait for her to leave. The one who didn't wait was Felisa. Before even five minutes had gone by, my intrepid assistant burst into the study and flung herself on my raised arm brandishing a syringe. When she saw her, Elsa jumped out of the armchair.

"Good Lord, Miss Plimsoll with her syringe!" she exclaimed, her mouth twisting into something halfway between a smile and a grimace.

"Come on, drop your trousers!" Felisa ordered. "You know you can't play games with me. You must excuse us, señorita, but it's urgent. His Highness here wants to duck out of it yet again, so he takes advantage of any visitors . . . He still won't accept the diagnosis, so what can we do?"

Drops of what I took to be inoffensive tap water dripped from the syringe, although the effect couldn't have been more dramatic. All I managed to stutter was:

"Just a moment, Felisa, just a moment . . ."

The debutante actress looked at me sorrowfully, rubbing her thighs and at a loss how to react. Terrified, she stared at Felisa and asked:

"What . . . what do you mean? Is there something wrong with him?"

"Better for you not to know, sweetheart. Have you ever heard of the pink plague? A nasty business." Turning to me once more, she barked: "Come on, trousers down, I haven't got all day! Keep away, señorita, please!"

Elsa Loris decided it was time to leave. She hastily apologised for disturbing us, expressing gratitude for my attention, and yet at the same time so confused that she improvised an effusive farewell, holding out her hand to me several times, but only offering her fingertips in what was no more than a wary gesture that the sly boots Felisa was not willing to let go unremarked.

"Don't worry, señorita. You can't catch it from contact or from saliva."

The poor girl made an attempt to smile, and then stood spontaneously on tiptoe to give me a quick peck on the cheek. I wholeheartedly wished her good luck and great success, and accompanied her to the door.

Afterwards I had to reprimand Felisa for her ridiculous, overbearing, gruesome and above all unnecessary intervention in defence of a perfect conjugal harmony that fortunately had always reigned in this house. Or almost always.

15

15

15

30. DELICIAS CINEMA. EXTERIOR. DAY.

Intermittent screech of tram wheels going down Torrente de las Flores, increasingly loud as it takes the bend at Travessera de Gràcia, opposite the cinema where Carol arrives twirling the green umbrella above her head. She stands gazing at the billboard announcing "Gilda" (the same crudely drawn poster from sequence 27, but now with the colours streaked and some tears in the canvas) that has been put on display again for this repeat showing of the film.

The drizzle has eased, and Carol closes the umbrella. She is eating roast chestnuts from a paper cone. She has on the grey beret and is without make-up, with high-heeled shoes, black stockings and a pair of red woollen socks. Shadows pass by her, occasionally propositioning her urgently with grunts that sound like snoring, but nobody comes to a halt. Or possibly they do, but she doesn't turn round to check. Not a single cheery wink of her almond-shaped eye, or any hint of a smile; she isn't looking for work in the street, or expecting to meet anyone. Raising the closed umbrella, she props it against her shoulder with a tired, awkward gesture as she continues to gaze up at the dazzling figure dominating the poster. The satiny love goddess is holding a smoking cigarette and languidly drags along a mink coat. She smiles suggestively, but in a rather cross-eyed way, perhaps because the rain has made the paint run; her magnificent mane of hair is torn at the level of her naked shoulder.

The fine rain comes on again and Carol opens the umbrella once more, throws the empty chestnut cone to the ground, turns on her heel and heads for the bar on the corner. She goes in (seen from the street through the steamed-up windows of the bar), approaches the counter and orders a glass of brandy, which she downs in one, pays for, and then leaves.

CUT to Lucas (aged 11, fists in pockets, patched trousers, his face half covered by a scarf) in the cinema foyer gazing at photographs in the glass panel. Carol closes her umbrella and quietly stands beside him. She seems somewhat unstable, dreamy. She stares at the boy in silence for a few seconds. At last she makes up her mind:

CAROL: Hello, little one. What are you doing here? (*With a complicit smile*) You haven't come to spy on your mother, have you?

Lucas glances suspiciously at her out of the corner of his eye.

CAROL: You'd like to see the film, wouldn't you? Or are you waiting to see if any strips of film are thrown out? Because there's a very pretty woman in that film, isn't there?

LUCAS: What's that to me? I like Tarzan movies. (*Suspiciously*) Hey, listen, I was only looking at the pictures. I'm not doing anything wrong.

CAROL (*with a friendly smile*): Of course not. But I could swear that what my boy wants is to see that film. Don't lie to me, now.

LUCAS (*shrugging*): What are you talking about? They won't let me in anyway!

CAROL (*lively, excited*): Why don't you sneak in? All the smart kids sneak in here. And you're smart, aren't you? Why don't you try? Come on. Mamma will help you!

LUCAS (*even more suspicious*): What do you mean?

Carol points to a staircase in a corner of the foyer.

CAROL: I've got a dodge. Can you see that staircase? I've got a friend waiting for me upstairs. As I'm going up, I'll call to the usher and say something to him, and he'll come straightaway because he's a very kind, friendly old man. That'll leave the entrance free. So then you can sneak in! What do you think of my plan, Dani, my love?

LUCAS: My name's Lucas . . . but . . . why are you crying?

CUT to Lucas crouching by the red plush curtain at the entrance to the stalls, about to sneak in. He smiles in grateful anticipation at Carol, who is chatting with the usher at the foot of the staircase. Carol says goodbye to the man and climbs the stairs to the door of the projection booth. She knocks, and while she is waiting takes off her beret, pats it, then puts it back on again. She raises her skirt slightly and adjusts the stocking and garter on her thigh.

The door opens, the film soundtrack booms out, and a smiling Sicart appears, wiping his hands on a greasy rag.

SICART: What took you so long, princess?

That word "princess" did not convince me at all, it didn't seem to fit in with the character, but Sicart had assured me that was what he usually called her. This made me wonder yet again about the false memory they could have introduced in the psychiatric hospital when they refashioned his past. I decided to keep this improbable term of affection simply for that reason, as the symptom of a hypothetical verbal implant that had nothing to do with his own earthier vocabulary; I would see later on if it fitted.

This was because I was now working on a fresh premise: meaning and atmosphere. I was extremely unhappy about the persistently chaotic sequencing, and had grave doubts that such an incoherent text without any clear objective could serve as the basis for the screenplay, but there was one thing I was sure of: the film wasn't in the police files or the records of the court proceedings, but in Fermín Sicart's impoverished, exploited memory, including his own reservations and mystifications.

I wouldn't be able to say what the limits of fiction are when it comes to recreating a historical truth; possibly the task is not to throw more light on the real event, but to emphasise the play of light and shade, the ambiguities and doubts, anything that contributes to the liveliest expression of the truth. I am able to say that some loose ends in such a fragmented tale added to its moral ambiguity, the fatalism of the characters, and even a climax of hidden violence, all of which were worthwhile elements because they fitted in with the character; and yet there was still the great question mark regarding the Big Bang of the terrible event: what motives coalesced at that initial moment, what was the seed of the first impulse, the starting point for the psychotic outburst that led Sicart to strangle the prostitute? And above all, why did I think that the account of the crime from the mouth of its protagonist was going to be so revealing and decisive? What was I hoping for from his explanation?

Sicart kept on postponing his repeated promise to tell me how he committed the crime because, according to his favourite excuse, before getting down to it he had to revise memories that, with the passage of the years and the readjustments imposed on him, were becoming confused and were fading. This excuse of a sleepwalking amnesia necessitated more sessions than I had planned – and extremely expensive ones, at five hundred pesetas an hour – which led me to suspect this was a ploy the sole aim of which was to increase his earnings . . .

One muggy evening in fitful sunshine I was busy sorting out the jammed tape recorder, and Sicart took advantage of the break to stretch his legs. He stood up with a glass of beer in his hand and was pacing round the terrace with a gloomy expression when I saw him come to a halt and peer up at the clouds.

"It was a day like today," he said. He shifted his tinted glasses to his forehead and went on: "Always threatening rain, until eventually it did come down."

Shortly before, early in the afternoon, a few spots of rain had fallen.

"Are you talking about the day of the crime?" I asked.

"I don't know, back then nearly every day was like it is today. Days when it rained on and off all day. At least, that's how I remember it," he said, as if apologising. "That's the impression I have, days of rain."

I waited to see if he was going to say anything more, but he didn't.

"Yes, that's right, it was raining. It's in the files."

"And the cinema was full, packed."

"So it must have been a holiday."

"No, it was a weekday, but you could hear from the booth that the stalls were jam-packed. I could hear the murmurs through the window, like cows ruminating."

"Cows?"

"Yes."

"Then Carol must have heard it too . . ."

He looked at me warily. With his index finger he slid his glasses down from his forehead to his nose.

"No," he said. "The only thing she heard was the voice of her son."

I could not get him to carry on.

"Did you ever get to know the boy?"

"No, but it was as if I had. She was always talking about her dead boy." He sat down again gloomily under the parasol and doused the cigarette butt in the beer glass. It took him several seconds to realise what he had done. "Damn, it must be true I have a screw loose! I thought it was the ashtray. I'm sorry."

"I'll tell Felisa to bring another beer."

"No, don't worry, there's some left in the bottle."

He poured the contents of the glass into the nearest flower-pot.

"That thing with Carol and her dead son was really sad," he said. "I told you about it the other day, do you remember? She was talking to the boy and let Señor Augé's budgerigar loose. And it had started to rain. Now I come to think of it, the first time she came to see me in the cinema it was raining, and so it was the last time as well."

Rain was not the only thing that kept coming back time and again in his devastated memory. During both of Carol's visits, the first and the last, with a gap of two years between them, the same film was being shown at the Delicias. I almost thought of implanting a false memory – a graft, a mere trick of memory designed to strengthen the plot with more echoes and resonances, a scene constructed with strands of verisimilitude to see if he took it on board, or at least considered it quite likely: his mother on her balcony furiously throwing another cage and another bird down into the street, definitively dismissing Liberto Augé from her emotional life just when Sicart was fervently wishing he had a father at home . . . I decided, however, to concentrate on the crime, and switched on the tape recorder without him noticing.

"So on that day Carol talked to her dead son," I said. "But why did she throw the cage into the street?"

"I don't know. Just before that she was telling me Encarnita was refusing to go and see an ophthalmologist." He smiled as he recalled this. "It seems the man had a glass eye, and Encarnita used to say: 'How can you trust an ophthalmologist with a glass eye!' Poor thing, she was very stubborn but not very bright, and Carol was worried about her. Well, after that, Carol began to rummage about for strips of film, and didn't want to eat. That was when she climbed onto the chair and opened the skylight." His gruff voice fell as the memory engulfed him. "Yes, that was when it all began . . ."

The perpetration of the crime, that presumably irrational, motiveless impulse that led to the murder, the moment of its creation, was about to be calmly evoked in Sicart's own voice, in a gravelly monotone that took him back to the past. In my mind, I had morbidly and self-indulgently recreated what I was about to hear, and was reserving for myself the pleasurable right to reinforce the climax of the whole affair with some apocryphal images of my own invention, but in the end I decided to keep the account without any alteration, exactly as it was recorded.

"How about we start from the beginning?" I suggested. "From the moment you open the door to the booth for her."

"The fact is, there's not a lot to tell. Everything happened so fast." He thought for a while. "Let's see . . ."

"Did you know where Carol was coming from that evening?"

"I never asked her where she was coming from, or where she was going."

"She was coming from the police station with Ramón Mir. According to his testimony, he stayed waiting for her in the bar on the corner, and he was there when you sent her out for some rolls."

"So what? What's that got to do with it?"

"There's a plausible hypothesis that can be deduced from several testimonies. Carol, who was a police informant and obeyed instructions from her lover, the Falangist Mir, had tracked down and denounced Liberto Augé, a wanted activist in the banned C.N.T., and intended also to denounce other members of the clandestine union. The C.N.T. became aware of this and you, very angry with her because of the damage she had done to Señor Augé, fell in with the C.N.T.'s plan, in other words, you agreed to do away with her."

"What on earth are you saying?" Sicart interrupted me. "I couldn't have cared a shit about the C.N.T. That's a story made up by the Politico-Social Brigade, my friend! Besides, I always trusted Carol, always, as I've already told you."

"Alright. Let's go back to the beginning. Did Carol turn up unannounced, or had you arranged to meet?"

Sicart took a few seconds to calm down.

"She usually came during the interval, at snack time. I had just switched on the house lights and was showing slides with local adverts."

"Had she been drinking?"

"Yes, but no more than on other occasions."

"Do you remember how she was dressed?"

"She was wearing . . ." Disturbed, he fell silent, then pushed his fingers under his glasses to rub his eyes, almost immediately staring into the distance above the surrounding roofs. "Look, if you think I feel bad telling the story again, you're mistaken. Not a bit of it. It would be weird if it affected me after all these years . . . I can assure you it all happened very naturally . . ." He reached for the bottle of beer on the table, but did not drink from it. "Well, let's see, what did you ask me? Oh, yes. She was wearing her raincoat and black stockings. She had already taken everything else off."

"I mean when she came in from the street."

"Oh, that I don't know. Sometimes she used to wear the grey beret. I remember that because before she kissed me she used to set it to one side." He stared into the distance once more, lost in thought. "She must have had an umbrella that day, because it was raining."

The orange light captured beneath the parasol hurt his eyes and so, as he surveyed the horizon beyond the city roofs, he half closed them, as if to repel a blinding reflection or an illusion that was too bright and persistent, even if only in memory.

"You argued about something that day: was there some problem?"

"Well, the projection of the film was interrupted twice. But the second time I wasn't in the booth, I'd made off." He took several swigs from the bottle. "The thing with the bird happened earlier. I could sense something was going on, because while she was taking off her clothes she never stopped looking at the budgerigar's cage. She climbed onto the chair and opened the skylight; she said it was very hot. I was checking the arc lamps, but saw her pick up the cage and start whispering things to the budgerigar. I asked her to close the window because it was raining, but instead she opened the cage and set the bird free. Just like that. I was really angry. I made her jump down from the chair and I shouted at her, I told her she was crazy, that what she had done was wrong, because Señor Augé was very fond of his little budgerigar. That was when she said to me: "Dani asked me to set him free, and I couldn't say no." Dani was her son, the boy who died of consumption when he was eleven."

"I know. What happened next?"

"She was very sad. She picked up the bottle of wine and started watching the film through the front window. For quite a while, she didn't say anything, simply drank. She had barely had any of the coffee and hadn't even touched her sandwich. I tried to cheer her up, but it was no use. Normally when she was drunk she liked to fool around a bit, but that day she was like another person. She looked so wretched – huddled between the two projectors, hair wet from the rain and her face pressed against the glass – that I draped the raincoat round her shoulders. It was because of all this that I was distracted and forgot about the projector . . . We must have been on the third reel when I heard whistling and stamping from the stalls. I corrected the focus, but then the sound went out of sync, there was a flash, and Carol got scared. I stopped the film and switched the house lights on. When I saw her with the soda siphon in her hand, all ready to save me from the flames, I burst out laughing, but that wasn't the end of it: the razor blade I used to scrape the splices in the film had disappeared, and she showed it to me jokingly, gesturing as if she were going to slit her wrists, and laughing in a way I didn't like at all. Normally it didn't take me more than two minutes to splice the film together, but she had distracted me for longer than I thought, and in my haste I chopped the film carelessly and lost quite a long piece, which I threw under the table."

He was saying all this slowly, almost as if his voice were

in slow motion, as if he needed to reassert himself, to hear himself telling the story again.

"So then," he said, "she picked up the length of film from the floor, began to look at the frames against the light, and said: 'My, she's still got her clothes on.' She hung the length of film round her neck and . . . came up to me in that way of hers . . . as if . . ."

Struggling with his frozen memory, Sicart turned round when he saw Felisa arrive with a tray and two bottles of beer that neither of us had asked for. Then, as though sensing a change in the atmosphere, in the failing evening light or in the vibration of the air, he fell silent and his head drooped.

"I thought you could do with something cool," Felisa said. She left the tray on the table, took a pair of secateurs out of her housecoat pocket, and walked away, saying: "I'm going to cut back the bougainvillea."

"That's how it was," Sicart said, picking up the thread of his thoughts. "I mean, she came towards me with the raincoat open. It was old, a man's raincoat. As I told you, she was wearing only that, and a pair of black stockings."

After that he lingered on details I'll omit here, erotic fantasies sublimated by memory. According to him, Carolina Bruil was a real expert at offering herself standing up, incredibly affectionate, warm and enveloping, and she always found some strange and exciting new variant. What she herself most enjoyed was for Sicart to kiss her neck. He was proud of the fact that he did everything she asked without spoiling her very expensive nylon stockings, and without at any point neglecting the projection, especially when she opened her legs for him.

"O.K., we can skip that kind of detail," I said. "I'm more interested in what you said to each other, and what happened next."

Sicart gave me a disappointed look.

"Right. You're only interested in the criminal act. The thing is, the two things happened at almost the same time, the criminal act and the coitus, if you'll excuse the term."

"I understand, but you see, what's important is something else. It's the impulse you couldn't control. Whatever it might have been, something led you to hang that length of film round her neck, and then . . ."

"But it wasn't me! I've already told you, she was the one who hung it round her neck!"

"Alright, it was her."

"She pretended it was a necklace, and joked: 'I'm Dame Necklace of the Delicias Cinema . . .'"

"By the way, did you know that on that same evening people saw Carol in the bar on the corner when she went to get rolls and beer with the length of film round her neck?"

"That doesn't surprise me." He concentrated again, rubbing the back of his hands. "She liked to show off. Well, so she looked at me sadly and said something about the rain, because it was raining."

"What did she say? Can you remember?"

"Something silly about how when she was a little girl she was scared of the rain. Poor Carol. People liked her, but the fact is she didn't have much gumption. She was worth her weight in gold, but was totally unaware of it. Do you know how much she charged for a trick when I first met her? Twelve pesetas and the price of the bed. I convinced her to ask for fifteen, and she was worth a lot more . . . when she hadn't been drinking, of course. And it wasn't because of the things she could do in bed, although she was very good at that – you can't imagine how good she was – no, it was because . . . Well, because when you told her about yourself, she listened in a way that was . . . different. I don't know how to explain it."

He said that he had no idea whether she behaved the same way with all her clients, or only with him.

"You liked her a lot, I can tell," I said. "But what happened then?"

"She bent down and picked up the length of film from the floor, and . . ."

He fell silent again, peering down at the ground. I could see it too: the length of celluloid about to become the murder weapon was there, on the tiles of the terrace: it was nothing more than a curl of film, a sleeping, harmless black caterpillar. Even when it was wrapped round Carol's neck it still seemed harmless.

"She picked it up and wound it round her neck," Sicart said.

"She had played at using the razor blade to cut her veins, and now she played at strangling herself with the film. She even stuck her tongue out. And as you can imagine, I didn't find that funny at all. She was quite crazy that day. The whole time she kept toying with her garters and stockings, which was all she had on. I don't know at what point I realised almost twenty minutes had gone by and I had to change reels, so I told her to sit down and finish the coffee. It was then, while I was checking the reels, that she came up to me with the raincoat over her shoulders, twisting the film round and round her neck."

He was talking without looking at me, shielded by his dark glasses and slowly stroking the palms of his hands, first one and then the other, as if that might help him retrieve the memory.

"I had started the other projector," he said. "I went over to her next to the first aid box, under the skylight that she had left open. From time to time I could feel the drizzle on my face. I took her from behind, and pushed her against the wall." Sicart pulled a face and bit his lip. "No, let's see, that's not what I wanted to tell you, it's something else. It's something I felt when we were doing it, but it has nothing to do with fucking, it was something else I can't explain. We were in between the two projectors, and I suddenly felt a hot wave spread over me. I don't know what went through my mind, but I'm sure I wanted to remove the length of film because I could see it was hurting her neck, there were already one or two cuts on her skin . . . I didn't cut my hands though because I was wearing gloves ... so that could have been the reason why ... the reason why I ..."

Bewildered, searching for the words, he snatched off his glasses and rubbed his eyelids. He wasn't pretending, he was really suffering.

"Well, let's leave it there for now, it's not important ..."

"The thing is, that celluloid scarf was in the way," he said, without hearing me. "I can clearly remember I wanted to kiss her on the neck but couldn't, and that was when she said to me in a whisper: 'Hurry up.' I'm not sure if I had already decided to do what I was going to do, I can't remember that, I only remember I knew what I was doing, I mean I was aware of it, I'm not looking for excuses . . . I suppose I didn't ease off until she collapsed by the projector, but I'm not sure of that either. That's because all of a sudden I found myself somewhere else, sitting in the back row of the stalls with no idea of how I had got there or what had happened."

With that he fell silent and looked at me without moving, tense and more expectant than I was: was he hoping for my approval of his long-awaited account? The first shadows of evening obscured his face and it wasn't easy to guess what he was thinking, but his rigid pose seemed to be saying: Now it's for you to explain what happened to me, what moved my hands, it's up to you to assign me the role I am to play in this ill-fated story; you, the celebrated author of fictions, you who claim to dig deep into the emotional processes that lie behind our behaviour and who is rewarded for that; you who are a master of the art of imagining reasons of the heart that reason is unaware of; it's up to you now to explain to me how and why and where that sudden, unfathomable aberration came from, an aberration that ruined my life.

When he saw me lower my head – I was pretending to take a sudden interest in whether the tape recorder was working properly – he perhaps thought that this was my way of expressing my frustration after all I had been hoping for, and said:

"I don't know if that's what you were expecting to hear. No doubt you imagined something different, and it's come as a blow to you. But that's what happened, and I don't think I've forgotten anything. As far as the motive is concerned, we haven't got any further, I'm afraid."

"It doesn't matter," I swiftly reassured him. "For the film they want, I think the motive matters least of all. As I told you, the director has other priorities."

"Oh, I see."

He took off his glasses to clean them on his handkerchief, and I could see his drained, lifeless eyes. It had grown dark in the past few minutes, so I got up to close the parasol. Sicart gulped down the rest of his beer and also stood up, wishing me goodbye until the following day. In one corner of the terrace, Felisa had finished cutting back the bougainvillea and was sweeping up the withered flowers with a brush and pan. When she saw that Sicart was about to leave, she kept him back for a few seconds, saying she would accompany him to the door, and, while she was finishing sweeping up, explained that this job of tidying the bougainvillea was what she liked best of all those she did on the terrace, because it got rid of all the old, useless vegetation, the wilted, parched flowers, and in that way helped the bougainvillea with its mute efforts to grow.

"Something that, looking around," she said without any apparent hint of mockery, "it's just occurred to me would also be useful to do with some men I've known."

But Sicart did not find this funny. Standing at the edge of the terrace, he was contemplating the first lights of evening winking on in the city, and seemed to be listening to the distant rumble of traffic from the streets below. He lit a cigarette, pulled the raincoat round his shoulders, took out the small comb he kept in his top pocket, and drew it through his thinning hair. He waited patiently for Felisa to finish sweeping up, and then docilely allowed her to accompany him to the front door.

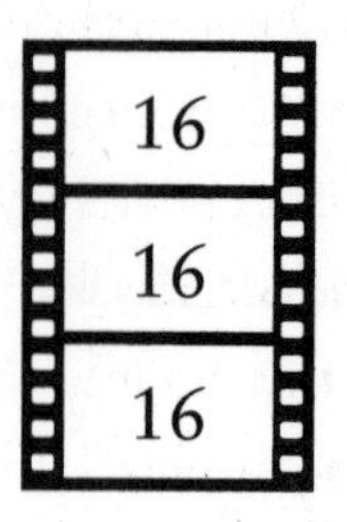

Simply to satisfy the producer's cheap hopes for the blind prostitute, and of course without having any idea of the consequences, I sketched out three new scenes that put her in the spotlight. I had to hold my nose to complete the last of these, one that revolved around an improbable, kind-hearted Encarnita full of good intentions, who has dealings with an equally improbable handicapped employee in the offices of the Blind Society, thanks to whose intervention she is finally given her longed-for guide dog.

I sent everything to Madrid, and while I was waiting for the go-ahead from Edgar Mardanos, went through the whole text with Sicart, who considered his story to be effectively complete. In this final revision, my uneasy conscience at all the concessions I had made to such an artificial character as the sweet little blind girl made me want to be stubbornly truthful and punctilious about the description of Sicart's working life. I wanted to know the precise details of his job, his surroundings and the urban environment.

"So they can use that famous phrase 'based on a true story'," I joked with Sicart. "That's a fallacy. But we'll have to give Encarnita a false name. What about Carmelita? Or Milagritos?"

"No, don't do that," Sicart said. "She would have liked to see her own name on it . . . Well anyway, it doesn't matter, the poor thing must be dead by now."

I had written sixty-seven double-spaced pages, with a few ideas for dialogue in some scenes, and even suggestions for the running order and sets. None of this was any of my business, but I felt like doing it. The first section was a compilation of the family, work and emotional experiences of victim and murderer; the second an objective account of how the crime had been committed.

By now it was mid-August, and I was counting the days until Carmen came home with the children. This was originally planned for the 23rd, but precisely the day before, Borja, the little brat spoilt rotten by his mother, had fallen off his bike as he rode along Utrechtsestraat, leaving him with a sprained ankle and a cracked rib, which meant that Carmen postponed her return to the end of the month.

At the start of the last week of August, things began to accelerate. On Monday 26, I had a thorough clear-out. I got rid of my recordings, photocopies and notes, spent a couple of hours sprawled on the sofa listening to Ben Webster's sax and reading in the local press a surprisingly honest and enthusiastic article about the transition they were cooking up in Madrid, then went for a swim.

There was no-one in the pool, and, as I swam a length, I found myself missing Señora Falp and her mocking grin as she overtook me with her stylish crawl, so slow and determined that now it seemed to me like an act of kindness, a discreet token of support for my troubles. It was as if she too were tracing in the water lines of writing that vanished almost instantaneously, and so had to be patiently reconstructed by means of a persistent, unwavering swimming action: the elbow slowly emerging from the water, the scrawny arm unhurriedly rising and re-entering time after time, the repeated, precise and syncopated way of revealing just one side of the face, concealing it beneath the surface and then immediately showing it again in the cadence of effort, the sustained rhythm and constant striving in search of an ephemeral kind of beauty or harmony. All that, I told myself as I swam alone, is mirrored by the movement of the sentence, resolutely deciphering an enigma on a sheet of paper, the persistence of memory over the passage of time, and the unexpected twist reality assumes the moment it has been grasped.

Once, as I turned, I caught sight of a red gleam at the bottom of the pool and instinctively dived underwater, imagining I could hear the thud of water stirred up by the expert swimmer's flashing feet. I went down a couple of metres and there it was, lurking behind a whirl of bubbles that must only be continuing to rise in my brain: the intermittent glint of the ruby. The earring had got caught in a crack in the drain, and although I tried desperately, pulling at it as hard as I could and rising several times to the surface to get my breath back before diving down again, I was unable to release it.

As I was leaving, I told the receptionist that Señora Falp had lost an earring in the pool. They said they would look into it at once, but told me that the earring couldn't possibly belong to Señora Falp, as she had quit the club almost a month earlier.

That same afternoon, shortly before Sicart arrived, Edgar Mardanos rang to tell me that Vilma Films Inc. had come to an agreement with the director J. L. de Prada for him to take over the definitive script and direct the film, and above all, he said, to thank me: the new scenes involving the blind whore were very good.

"Prada really liked them," he said. "So much so that he thinks the script will need to be revised quite a lot, and wants complete control over it from now on. He'll be in touch with you this week."

The best news was, Mardanos said, that the project was definitely on track. Vilma Films Inc. was benefiting from the new legislation on subsidies introduced by the National Film Board, based on the French model. This meant that production expenditure would increase by 25 to 30 per cent, so the budget would be between 50 and 70 million pesetas. In fact, the film had already been sold, a distribution deal had been done, so if we didn't want to miss out on the funds we had to start pre-production at once. Still euphoric, Mardanos insisted on the relevance and value of the initial treatment, "even if one ought to take some of the director's suggestions into account". The most important of these was to slightly shift the focus of the narrative to the blind prostitute, because he saw an extraordinary potential for tenderness and sympathy in her character, which would be ideal to quickly establish a relationship of complicity and emotion with the audience, not to mention the touch of humour that, together with J. L. de Prada's recognised mastery as a director, was the company's trademark. "Fine, I get it," I muttered. Mardanos added that perhaps it would be worth entrusting Encarnita's dialogue to a writer of witty and to a certain extent poetic comedies, someone like Miguel Mihura, may he rest in peace . . . Of course, he hastened to point out, the original idea was still there: the plot revolved around the murder of the prostitute Carolina Bruil, and the proof was that for the final version Prada had suggested bringing in a scriptwriter of T.V. action films shot in fabulous locations on the Costa del Sol, had I seen any of them? No? Well, he would send me a copy, I would love them, they were the big hit of the moment. The protagonist was an attractive female Civil Guard lieutenant, an expert diver who solved drug trafficking cases swimming beneath the waters of the Straits of Gibraltar.

Señora Falp's sunken ruby was still sending me its red flashes, dammit!

"Prada sees it clearly," Mardanos went on. "The most important thing, what counts above all, is not the killer's inability to remember, but the lovable little whore's blindness . . . And mark my words: Encarnita will win heaps of fans. D'you know why? Because compared to the high-class whores, those celebrity nonentities who play themselves on T.V. for money and are praised by four cretins in the gossip magazines, Encarnita is a real heroine, an innocent, lovable creature. I could see the potential of that girl right from the start, d'you remember? And you didn't believe me. What do you say now?"

This was starting to annoy me.

"You already know my opinion. A blind whore is a character from fantasy fiction. But anyway, it's up to you."

"No, it's not that," Mardanos said. "At any rate, I know that Prada doesn't want to make her the main character. It's nothing more than a narrative strategy. He thinks Carolina Bruil's murder would be more interesting if we learn about it through the testimony of her friend Encarnita, who is so simple and lost, with the humorous slant she brings to the role. She's a tart with a heart of gold, who finds work despite her handicap. Her clients are solitary, ridiculous men, often damaged and deformed. All she dreams of is a guide dog. The public will love her from the start! Because we'll see the film told by her, by the voice and gaze of a sightless girl who is a delight. It's an interesting approach, isn't it?"

"Yes, maybe," I heard myself say. "But I wonder whether a prostitute who turns tricks in the Chinese quarter touching up cripples and weirdos or whoever she can because she is blind will really be delightful enough to seduce the public."

Marsano gave a silly, forced laugh, and then, the nerve of him, he actually said that this kind of dark, twisted humour was what José Luis de Prada most appreciated; he knew what ingredients a film needed to be a success. He added: "Do you remember that question Rossellini asked himself: should one look at things as they are, or should one pursue one's dreams? There you have it."

He insisted I had done an excellent initial treatment and, again employing the banal rhetoric of political language so fashionable in those days, he rounded off his praise with his favourite slogan:

"Now we all need to pull together. The final script demands it. And, of course, anything you can suggest will be gratefully received. We're still counting on you, your contribution isn't over yet."

I knew that it was. I was tempted to tell him: if it's suggestions you're after, here's one: if you want that cheerful, endearing blind whore to be believable, make sure she at least gives an unwitting dose of clap to the Blind Society official who offers her the guide dog, because there's always room for a spot of realism. In fact, what I said was:

"Oh, by the way, I'm still owed some money."

"I know. Vilches will take care of the details. But listen, this isn't goodbye, is it? We'll be in touch. So we'll see you soon."

At that moment neither of us could have known it (although Mardanos already had a firm hand on the puppet strings), but over the following months, Vilma Films Inc.'s ambitious project concerning the crime in the Delicias cinema did a complete U-turn, in such a random, bubbly way it would have brought a smile to the face of the sacked director Héctor Roldán. It ended up being the story of a failure. The original script, first championed by a combative director with tired eyes determined to burst the fetid bubbles of Francoism that to his mind were still floating unchecked in the air, was to pass through various hands, offices and budgets until it became a riotous, prophylactic sex romp that proved to be a huge box office hit entitled "Manolita's Blind Passions", a farce that had absolutely nothing to do with any real events and in which there was no strangled whore, no amnesiac murderer, and of course absolutely no memory, either individual or collective, that was worth recuperating or laying claim to, not even as a simple tribute to the truth.

The last meeting with Fermín Sicart under the parasol on the terrace took place one Saturday evening and went on until well after nightfall. When I told him our work was done, he became pensive, as if he had forgotten to tell me something and was struggling to remember what it was.

"So it's all over," he said, removing his sunglasses.

"Yes, that's what I've been told."

"Are you sure you won't want me anymore?"

"No. I think we have all the information we need."

"Are you sure?" he insisted. "Because last night I recalled a few things that I think might interest you."

"Thanks, but don't trouble yourself. You've been a real help, you know."

He fell silent and paid me no more attention. He looked so downhearted I didn't know how to bring things to a close, and so instead asked him to stay for supper. "Felisa will prepare an excellent gazpacho and then some prawns," I told him. He gazed at me as if he were looking straight through me, and apologised: he had somewhere to be. Yet more than half an hour went by and he couldn't bring himself to leave. I asked him to at least share a glass of cava with me before he left, assuring him Felisa would be upset if he refused, because it had been her idea and the bottle was already chilling. A faint smile appeared on his lips and, staring as he often did into the distance beyond the rooftops of a shadowy Guinardó, he said:

"At the bar in Panam's, whenever a generous client offered to buy her a drink, she always asked for champagne." He continued, gleefully celebrating the sudden rekindling of memory:

"In winter she would turn up at the cinema with a paper cone of roast chestnuts. And in summer, with lemon ice lollies. And she liked to go on the pleasure cruises round the port, and also . . . Just a minute, let me think: there were so many things she enjoyed."

He was quiet, staring anxiously into space and weighing up what he was about to say. It was obvious that before he left he wanted to offer me as a reward or a tip some previously untold memories he had of Carolina Bruil. And so it proved: all at once and in the best possible humour he launched into a hasty description of the whims or personal eccentricities of his beloved. He seemed to have memorised them beforehand and was offering me them in case they might still be useful for the film.

"As well as roast chestnuts, she liked talking to children, sleeping in men's pyjamas, *Lucky* cigarettes, nylon stockings . . ." In a monotone, eyes closed, Sicart listed the flotsam from the shipwreck. "And a song as well, though I've forgotten the words . . . She had a birthmark just by her mouth, and another bigger one on her left thigh, and at night her breasts were like a warm stone, and nine was her lucky number, she always bought lottery tickets with nine in them."

Feeling faintly depressed by all this, I said:

"Please don't go to so much trouble; it's not worth it. It's clear to me that they don't want to know anything more, they've got all they need."

"I only wanted to be of use to you," he said softly. "That's all."

At that moment, seeing him accept my verdict with head bowed, I was suddenly aware of our defeat, his and mine: his because of his plundered past, dredged up and reconstructed, mine because I had been unable to do anything with those bits and pieces he had been left with and was unaware of, finally encoded in those two words Carolina Bruil uttered shortly before she died, whose meaning had been lost forever.

As if reading my mind, Sicart glanced at me apologetically.

"I know my memory is poor. I know I was a different person, not quite right in the head. But I don't know if I've been able to explain it to you. I don't think I have."

"Don't torment yourself; it's not worth it. It's not important anymore. As for the film, let's see what comes out of all this . . ."

At last Felisa appeared with the cava and two glasses. Sicart bestirred himself and offered to uncork the bottle, joking about the perilous way Felisa had startled him in one of our first sessions. Getting up from the table, he thanked Señora Felisa and me for all our kindness since his first appearance at our house, and celebrated the quips she had made, including the ones he had never understood. He insisted she fetch another glass to join us in toasting the success of the film.

"My memory isn't very good, but let's hope the film is," he said, raising his glass. "She would have liked that."

"Oh, I would as well," I said, not at all convinced.

In her habitual rather grumpy tone, Felisa added:

"Would you like the advice of an old grouch who does have a good memory, Señor Sicart?" She paused for a moment, sketched an affectionate smile, and said: "Whatever happens, don't take it too much to heart."

Sicart smiled back at her, but said nothing. Shortly afterwards he said a brief farewell, and I accompanied him to the front door. Before leaving, he adjusted the dark glasses on his nose and asked:

"What did Señora Felisa mean by saying I shouldn't take it to heart? Was that another of her damned riddles?"

"It could be," I told him. "Poor Felisa thinks that films solve life's riddles. And do you know something? Every so often I think she's right."

He nodded pensively. After he had gone, I went back to the terrace and leaned over the balustrade to watch him leave the building. He was standing on the edge of the pavement and the night, near a part of the street that was badly lit because of a faulty lamp on the corner. He stood there a few seconds, glancing one way and then the other as if he didn't know which direction to take. He lit a cigarette, flung the raincoat round his shoulders and finally headed towards the flickering streetlight. He walked deliberately, at no great pace, holding himself erect in a feigned, old-fashioned pose, shoulders and neck tense in a manner that suggested violence, a stiffening that was probably no more than affectation, but which even so somehow helped him keep his tryst with an impoverished, reconstructed and fateful past that he didn't know how to or want to relinquish, possibly because it was the only one he had.

THE END

JUAN MARSÉ is a Spanish novelist and screenwriter, born in Barcelona in 1933. Following the publication of his first novel in 1960, he has gone on to become one of his country's most respected and beloved authors. He has been honoured with many literary awards, including the European Literature Prize and the Cervantes Prize.

NICK CAISTOR is a translator, journalist and author. He has thrice been awarded the Premio Valle-Inclán for Spanish translation. His translations include works by Paulo Coelho, Eduardo Mendoza, Juan Marsé, Edney Silvestre and Dominique Sylvain.

A New Library from MacLehose Press

This book is part of a new international library for literature in translation. MacLehose Press has become known for its wide-ranging list of best-selling European crime writers, eclectic non-fiction and winners of the Nobel and Independent Foreign Fiction prizes, and for the many awards given to our translators. In their own countries, our writers are celebrated as the very best.

Join us on our journey to **READ THE WORLD**.

1. *The President's Gardens* by Muhsin Al-Ramli
TRANSLATED FROM THE ARABIC BY LUKE LEAFGREN

2. *Belladonna* by Daša Drndić
TRANSLATED FROM THE CROATIAN BY CELIA HAWKESWORTH

3. *The Awkward Squad* by Sophie Hénaff
TRANSLATED FROM THE FRENCH BY SAM GORDON

4. *Vernon Subutex 1* by Virginie Despentes
TRANSLATED FROM THE FRENCH BY FRANK WYNNE

5. *Nevada Days* by Bernardo Atxaga
TRANSLATED FROM THE SPANISH BY MARGARET JULL COSTA

6. *After the War* by Hervé Le Corre
TRANSLATED FROM THE FRENCH BY SAM TAYLOR

7. *The House with the Stained-Glass Window* by Żanna Słoniowska
TRANSLATED FROM THE POLISH BY ANTONIA LLOYD-JONES

8. *Winds of the Night* by Joan Sales
TRANSLATED FROM THE CATALAN BY PETER BUSH

9. *The Impostor* by Javier Cercas
TRANSLATED FROM THE SPANISH BY FRANK WYNNE

10. *After the Winter* by Guadalupe Nettel
TRANSLATED FROM THE SPANISH BY ROSALIND HARVEY

11. *One Clear, Ice-Cold January Morning at the Beginning of the Twenty-First Century* by Roland Schimmelpfennig
TRANSLATED FROM THE GERMAN BY JAMIE BULLOCH

12. *The Shape of the Ruins* by Juan Gabriel Vásquez
TRANSLATED FROM THE SPANISH BY ANNE McLEAN

13. *Vernon Subutex 2* by Virginie Despentes
TRANSLATED FROM THE FRENCH BY FRANK WYNNE

14. *Stick Together* by Sophie Hénaff
TRANSLATED FROM THE FRENCH BY SAM GORDON

15. *The Tree of the Toraja* by Philippe Claudel
TRANSLATED FROM THE FRENCH BY EUAN CAMERON

16. *The Oblique Place* by Caterina Pascual Söderbaum
TRANSLATED FROM THE SWEDISH BY FRANK PERRY

17. *Tropic of Violence* by Nathacha Appanah
TRANSLATED FROM THE FRENCH BY GEOFFREY STRACHAN

18. *My Name is Adam* by Elias Khoury
TRANSLATED FROM THE ARABIC BY HUMPHREY DAVIES

19. *E.E.G.* by Daša Drndić
TRANSLATED FROM THE CROATIAN BY CELIA HAWKESWORTH

20. *Katalin Street* by Magda Szabó
TRANSLATED FROM THE HUNGARIAN BY LEN RIX

21. *Balco Atlantico* by Jérôme Ferrari
TRANSLATED FROM THE FRENCH BY DAVID HOMEL

22. *Lord of All the Dead* by Javier Cercas
TRANSLATED FROM THE SPANISH BY ANNE McLEAN

23. *The Faculty of Dreams* by Sara Stridsberg
TRANSLATED FROM THE SWEDISH BY DEBORAH BRAGAN-TURNER

24. *The Archipelago of Another Life* by Andreï Makine
TRANSLATED FROM THE FRENCH BY GEOFFREY STRACHAN

25. *The Last Days of El Comandante* by Alberto Barrera Tyszka
TRANSLATED FROM THE SPANISH BY ROSALIND HARVEY AND JESSIE MENDEZ-SAYER

26. *The Snares of Memory* by Juan Marsé
TRANSLATED FROM THE SPANISH BY NICK CAISTOR